I0639030

Restless Echoes

A ghostly dog, a strange lady and the confused memories of a young girl are about to complicate Polly, Sarah and Clarrie's lives.

Unravelling the different mysteries is going to need all of them working together and it is likely to put the family and their circle of friends at risk.

Not only must they solve two horrific crimes, they need to find a murderer before he strikes again.

Also by Mai Griffin

Deadly Shades of Grey is now 'Ghostly Echoes'
A Poisonous Shade of Grey is now 'A Poisonous Echo'
Grey Masque of Death is now 'Dangerous Echoes'
Haunting Shades of Grey is now 'Haunting Echoes'
This book 'Restless Echoes' is the last in the series

Somebody Came (Stand-alone)

First published in Great Britain in 2018 by U P Publications
Registered Office: St George's House, George Street,
Huntingdon, Cambridgeshire, UK PE29 3GH

Cover design copyright © U P Publications 2020

Copyright © Mai Griffin 2018

Mai Griffin has asserted her moral rights

A CIP Catalogue record of this book is available from the British Library

This edition ISBN 978-1-912777-00-6
eBook ISBN 978-1-912777-01-3

FIRST PAPERBACK EDITION

Published by U P Publications

www.uppbooks.com
www.maiwriting.com
www.maigriffin.com

Restless Echoes

Mai Griffin

U P PUBLICATIONS
2018

In Life and Death there is no Black and White,
No core construct that always must be right,
No path or light that clearly shows the way
But filters through a Deadly Shade of Grey.

When some can hear and others single sight
How can they find a soul to lead them to the light?
Ghostly Echoes make confusion and tend to disarray,
So pander to the madness of what the seers say

In Death's dark realm, where none of us may stray,
The light glints through a Poisonous Shade of Grey.
A Glimmer glimpsed, beyond a heart's endeavour,
Where lost souls wander in their dark forever.

A soul that's lost in Death's last cunning sway
Can still fright the living from the depths of their decay.
A Poisonous Echo, sent by the unforgiving,
Reaches out, with hate, to scar and maim the living.

Now mourners gather, to share a lasting glance,
Where grief full memories perform a final dance
and movement stills, as with departing breath,
the music plays the last Grey Masque of Death

As each note rises, to reach its audience
The spirits strain to meet each consequence
When souls conspire to circumvent the truth
Their Dangerous Echoes ululate sans ruth.

Ghostly movements flicker through the night,
Where mortals peer and seek to soothe their fright,
The living lost far from the light of day,
Where shadows play their Haunting Shades of Grey.

The Haunting Echoes of lives long lost
Resonate without a single thought to cost.
Revenging wraiths seek living dreams to claim,
And guilty souls who need to take their blame

Buildings loom, stark, cloaked in white
And ruined windows blink, transfixed by pale moonlight
Rustling shadows flutter and, windless, sway
As night gives way to Ghostly Shades of Grey

Long lost spirits seek to find their past,
Locked in a purgatory they themselves have cast,
With earthly ties they cannot seem to sever,
Restless Echoes mock their last endeavour

Anon

1. The Kitchen Lady

Remembering what had happened the last time she had involved Sarah in her family problems, Polly was reluctant to do so again. "I'm really sorry, but no!" She gripped the telephone tightly, to emphasise how determined she was, "Sarah deserves a rest, and anyway, she never goes looking for ghosts – enough of them come back to bother her anyway, without her giving them any encouragement." Polly flatly refused to ask any favours, even for her son-in-law.

Gavin was upset, of course. He protested, "But I've known Dave for years, dammit – we were at school together. His son's new house is haunted, and he's really scared..." He paused when Polly interrupted his flow, and then replied, offended, "Of course I haven't told him about *'Psychic Sarah'* – I promised not to gossip about her, and I never have."

"Really, Gavin, there's no need to be disrespectful," said Polly. "You have to understand that Sarah is not as young as she was and has acceded to very few requests since all the trauma when Clarrie was attacked."

"She must be well over that by now, and..."

"...And," Polly interjected firmly, "there are dozens of mediums advertising their skills, who would welcome the publicity if they rid the house of ghosts. On the other hand, he could ask his vicar's advice."

Despite her refusal to intercede, Polly was intrigued. She could not resist asking why Dave's son and his wife were convinced their house was haunted and with little encouragement, Gavin explained. As soon as they moved into their newly built home, Dave's son, Pete and daughter-in-law, Peggy, fancied they heard movements in parts of the house where they were sure the rooms were empty. They attributed the noises to settlement or new timber flooring, or just about anything normal, not discussing even the remote possibility that they were supernatural.

Only when the children, talking to each other, referred to things *the lady* had said or done, did they begin to take more notice. The children had few adult friends, and all were known to their parents – so who, they wondered were *Toby, Annie* and *Babs*? Their own children, Andy, Amy and Holly, had never had a problem playing together although at seven years old Andy always assumed the role of leader, dictating what game they would play.

One day, Peggy heard Andy asking the baby of the family to choose. Holly, was only four, and refused. "You must," said Andy. "The Kitchen Lady says it's not fair if you never have a turn." Only then did the young couple begin to worry, when their children spoke of the strange woman and other things, in complete acceptance of their existence.

Holly cried one day when she couldn't find her favourite doll. Her sister, a year older, reminded her that the Kitchen Lady took it from her because it had fallen onto the wet floor. Andy added that the lady put it in the airing cupboard to dry. It was, of course, found in the airing cupboard. Even more disconcerting: the two little girls were used to having a bedtime story and one night, when their mother went to tuck them up and started to read to them, they said the lady had read that bit to them already – could they hear the next page please? She questioned them about the story and was in no doubt that they knew more than she had read to them herself.

Polly commented that many children could read at the age of five or even three – it was even possible that their brother had read it aloud for them. In fact, the three children could be carrying out what, to them, would be a funny prank. It was a fair comment, Gavin agreed, but his friends weren't stupid; other things had happened, of a more sinister nature, which were quite definitely not attributable to childish pranks.

He refused to say more, still upset by Polly's refusal to help him. Sensing that she had, perhaps, been a little too dismissive, Polly finally promised that she would mention it casually to Sarah, if an opportunity arose – not asking her to help, of course, but she would let Gavin know if Sarah made any useful comments.

Gavin Bishop had been happily married to Jane, Polly's daughter, for over twenty years and, in all that time had abided by Sarah's desire for privacy. He never discussed her or the way she sometimes helped the police with their enquiries – in a non-criminal way of course, he grinned wryly at his private joke. He had never, ever, asked a personal favour. He should have approached Sarah directly, he thought, not asked Polly to intercede; she was always over-protective of her erstwhile employer. Being life-long friends and now her live-in companion did not give Polly the right to censor messages or special requests!

He was fond of his mother-in-law – they were on the best of terms, but he was determined that Sarah should hear about his friend's problem. Whatever she advised him to do, he would accept. If anyone other than his mate, Dave, had told him about the haunting, Gavin wouldn't have believed it, but they had been at school together and he could tell Dave was genuinely scared for his family's safety. Apart from anything else, one or other of Gavin's two younger daughters often baby-sat for the three children; he certainly did not want them to be scared half to death.

Gavin was determined to tell Sarah, if Polly didn't. Dave's description of what he had witnessed personally was frightening. In the meantime, if they needed a baby-sitter, he would have to volunteer himself!

2. At Home

Sarah Grey had carried on walking to the garden, when Polly indicated that the phone call was not for her, but she'd heard the beginning of the conversation. She understood Polly's concern, but she really must have a word with her – the terrible time was well past! The last few years had actually been enjoyably quiet, and Sarah had again settled into her bridge mornings, dinners with friends and catching up on books unread. Perhaps it was time to stop being so self-indulgent.

They had just enjoyed a visit from Clarinda and her husband Del, who preferred staying for weekends rather than making one-day round-trips on busy roads. Having time with the baby was such a joy – especially as Emma was just beginning to talk. They lived only forty miles away, so it was not too far for Polly to drive when they needed a change of scene, or to babysit on rare occasions when Clarinda's painting commissions took her away from home for several working days. Their pet dachshund was a great help on such occasions; he lay on the mat outside the nursery door and rushed to bark the house down as soon as Emma stirred.

As much as she loved the family, Sarah enjoyed her quiet life at home. The gentle exercise of weeding the rockery for an hour in the afternoon sunshine calmed her. It had rained during the morning, so she was keen to take advantage of the loosened soil. Having showered, resting with a book passed another hour, so it was not until after dinner that Sarah remembered to ask Polly about Gavin's problem. She knew that his daughters sometimes babysat for a friend's grandchildren and guessed that the friend must be Dave. Polly was aware that Sarah had overheard part of her conversation, so she first confirmed that the person with a problem was the son of Gavin's oldest friend. Polly had met Dave but didn't really know his family...

Sarah agreed with Polly that they couldn't dismiss the idea that the children might be playing tricks on their parents, but Polly explained that there were more alarming incidents. Gavin would be able to describe the situation better, to them both, if Sarah had time to see him. Of course, Sarah agreed – she was always willing to help when asked. Tuesday was not one of her busy days, so they agreed that Gavin could bring Dave round for a drink and a chat, at about six-o-clock the following day.

Gavin was delighted when Polly rang to invite him, with or without Dave. He contacted Dave, immediately, telling him that both his mother-in-law and Sarah had encountered similar circumstances and might therefore be able to offer advice, but he decided not to mention that Sarah was psychic.

As always, at the prospect of another investigation, Polly's thoughts were churning – excitedly anticipating how Sarah would tackle the problem and how she would be able to help. Sarah, quietly enjoying her coffee as she watched the news on TV, was quite happy to ignore the issue until she knew more.

An hour later, after watching a quiz show together, Polly couldn't resist the subject any longer and had a suggestion to make. "I know where Dave's son lives. I could drive you to see the area tomorrow morning ...it might help if you could see the estate before you hear more about the haunting. What do you think?"

Sarah was not deceived – in spite of Polly's initial protests, she was, as always, eager to get to grips with any new problem. Her practical approach and support had proved invaluable in the past, so Sarah did not have the heart to refuse; it might even be a good idea.

They decided to have an early night, so that they could drive around the estate before the working day started. Who knew what might emerge from the morning gloom?

3. Things Heard and Seen

Although Clarinda had married and had made a new home with Del, she still owned the house where Sarah and Polly lived. When Sarah's husband died (and she'd sold the family home in Berkshire) Sarah would have been happy to buy an apartment of her own. Instead, Sarah and Polly moved to Oxfordshire to help Clarinda, still struggling to come to terms over the recent loss of her first husband. Now, years later and remarried, it had been time for Clarinda to move on.

Over the years, Sarah had become so accustomed to everyone else calling her Clarrie that sometimes she did too. Sarah's sisters, Clare and Linda, whose names had been combined, had both now died ...so it hardly seemed to matter, if it ever had, which of their names was the more prominent.

Without question, Polly stayed with Sarah. Much of their past was shared and they had so many memories in common that they were comfortable living together. When Clarrie married Del and left them, to be with him nearer to Oxford where he was based, Sarah and Polly would have been happy to move on, but Clarrie persuaded them to continue living in her house.

It held so many happy memories for her but, more importantly and, she admitted, totally selfishly, she and

Del would never find a lovelier house to live in when they retired. It had no near neighbours and the wide, sweeping driveway allowed for plenty of parking space without blocking the small amount of passing traffic.

Clarrie persuaded them that they would be doing her a favour and, secretly, they were both a little relieved and happy to agree. Although prepared for change, they were both a little daunted at the thought of having to pack up and find somewhere new, even though they didn't feel their age. They had grown fond of the old house and enjoyed its space and privacy. Plus, the extra income from Sarah's invested sale proceeds from selling her Berkshire property gave them a feeling of security they were loath to lose.

Before she left, Clarrie had refurbished her old painting studio as an office with a comfortable double bed-settee that would serve as a guest room when needed. Although Polly had her laptop computer she was ecstatic when Clarrie installed a complete range of machines in the new office, including printers and a scanner. They had a strong broadband connection and the strategic use of cables gave Polly's laptop access to the internet in the sitting room, but Sarah preferred using the desktop computer and Polly still borrowed it when she wanted to use the printer.

Sarah loved surfing the internet for information, never ceasing to be amazed at how much could be discovered online. She was comfortable with emails but still preferred to compose letters as documents, which she either printed and posted or sent as attachments.

On Tuesday morning, Polly emerged from the office

as Sarah's bedroom door opened. "Don't leave the computer on for me today, Polly, thanks," Sarah said, "I'd rather go now, if you've finished."

"Fine," Polly grinned, "I'm glad you're eager, but breakfast is ready to be served ...and no – it won't keep until we get back," she added, leading the way downstairs. Polly, although older, still insisted on doing most of the cooking and overseeing the housekeeping. Many times, she had seen Sarah totally exhausted, after coping with the amazing cases that came her way. She regarded it as her role in life to make sure, in between, that Sarah's life was as serene as possible.

Half an hour later they were ten miles outside the town centre, driving along a wide road, approaching the lane that led to the estate. They encountered very little traffic and, within minutes, had entered a leafy lane, which led to the farmhouse. Just before they reached it, they turned off onto a newly tarmacked road with an assortment of different styled dwellings on each side.

Several adjoining roads carried traffic through the rest of the estate, which had been visible from the motorway. Once cattle had grazed on the grassy field that separated them. In the old days the lane used to turn at the farmhouse, through what was left of the agricultural land, to the terraced labourers' cottages.

Sarah commented that it was nice to see a new estate where the houses were not all the same. There were no walls separating the front gardens from the pavements and all the garage doors were a different colour. Polly thought the effect was bizarre but admitted it must make it easier to issue directions for deliveries and visitors to parties.

Gavin's directions were clear, and, after several turns, they soon spotted the house – the family home of Dave's son. It was on a boundary of the estate, almost at the end of the road. A small patch of wasteland separated it from the last half-dozen houses on their side ...fortunately not big enough, or private enough, to attract local gangs! On all sides of the estate, there were woodlands or open fields, and their property was located on the perimeter farthest away from the main road, with views of the countryside beyond; there seemed no reason why it, alone, should be haunted.

Some garage doors were creaking open and a few cars passed by as Polly parked where they had a clear view of the whole corner without intruding on anyone's privacy. "Why have we stopped?" Sarah asked. "It was interesting to see the house and surroundings, but I really would rather leave now."

In an amazed tone, Polly replied. "But you asked me to pull over – I did think it was rather odd." One look made her realise that whatever she heard, it was nothing to do with Sarah. A few years ago, they discovered that Polly was clairaudient, but she had heard nothing out of this world since then. Now, instead of being worried, Polly was thrilled. "We can wait a little while, surely. There must be a reason for what I heard." Sarah agreed and laughingly suggested that they should sit quietly and await further instructions.

The next few minutes seemed like thirty, as the seconds dragged by. There had been no movement anywhere, since they stopped, although distant exhaust noises hung in the still air.

The day began to brighten slowly, and Polly was expecting Sarah to give up. She could see children moving inside the Fletcher property, but something more interesting must be happening because Sarah was holding her breath and her eyes seemed glued to an upper window. Eventually, Sarah relaxed, closed her eyes for a moment, and then said it was time to go. They drove back home in silence – Polly knew when not to ask questions and keep her thoughts to herself.

On arrival, she was pleased to see her niece's car parked on the far side of the driveway rather than anywhere near the double-garage door, which opened smoothly, responding to the remote control. Pat came to work every morning for a couple of hours since Polly had been persuaded to hand over the heavier chores, so coffee would be percolating, and they could settle quickly to chatting and planning.

Once inside, she and Sarah went to change, and both reappeared within minutes. Sarah smiled gratefully, as she joined Polly at the kitchen table, and was given a buttered scone with her drink. "Well, I'm not sure what all that was about," she said, "but it was a clever idea of yours. I'm glad we went. I saw nothing strange at first – until I realised that the dog I could see at the bedroom window was not a family pet."

Anticipating Polly's query, she said the children were clearly oblivious to the huge animal between them and the outside world. She had no idea what her vision meant but perhaps all would become clear when they met Dave. The day passed without further incident...

Pat always tackled the kitchen last, so Polly decided to stay out of Sarah's way and cook. Sausage rolls would go well with the beer the men were sure to want, later. Sarah received a call from Clarrie in the early afternoon, confirming that they were safely back home and then, later, a longer call from her friend Maud, even though they would be playing Bridge together the following morning.

Maud only ever gossiped over the phone ...too many ears around the tables, she averred. Before ringing off, she asked if Sarah's secret life was still quiet. Sarah knew what she meant.

Like all her close friends, Maud knew that she was psychic, but never referred to it other than obliquely ...after all, one never knew who was within hearing! She seemed obsessed by the idea that eager eavesdroppers were constantly after her secrets. Sarah never discussed such things anyway with friends, or indeed with anyone not directly involved, so escaped quickly by saying that guests were expected, and she had to go. Fortuitously, the doorbell sounded as she spoke, so her excuse was real.

The serenity Sarah displayed when Gavin introduced Dave belied her inner eagerness to hear Dave's story. Since seeing the ghostly dog, she was certain that it would not be a tissue of lies and hoped that she would be able to help him. She would certainly try.

4. Clarrie and Friend

After ringing her mother to enjoy discussing their visit, Clarrie settled down to paint. There were several hours of daylight left and plenty of time to cook dinner before Del came. She reflected on how her life had changed in the last few years. She was back to running her own home again, as she had during her first marriage. Del no longer urged her to employ help, knowing that she welcomed spells away from her easel and liked the freedom to stop and start tasks when it suited her.

Her studio adjoined the nursery, so Emma was no problem. As for the evening meal, she always prepared everything before she became too absorbed in her work and set the oven-timer to finish off their dinner. They never ate immediately on Del's arrival home – they enjoyed chatting over a drink beforehand, even if it meant Del's joining her in the kitchen, watching progress. His hours at the local *Investigator* were long, but at least he was not likely to have another assignment overseas – they were usually reserved for single correspondents.

Clarrie tutored a small group of students once a week. Her 'classroom', conveniently on the ground floor adjacent to the utility room, was easily accessible from the garden and would have accommodated more, but she restricted the class to five people so that she would have time to help each one with their individual problems, in the allotted three hours. If their only problems were with painting, life would be easy but, taking after her mother, Clarrie also was psychic, and she sometimes sensed their personal worries. Trying to convey the gist of any advice without revealing her source was always difficult.

Only a month ago, the long-dead grandmother of one woman would not fade away until Clarrie introduced the topic of headaches into the general conversation and drew an admission from the woman that she suffered almost daily. Everyone urged her to see her doctor and their assurances that it was unlikely to be a brain tumour, extracted a promise that she would make an appointment. The ghostly grandma nodded her thanks and disappeared, leaving Clarrie feeling responsible for following through – making sure that all went well.

A couple of years ago, her close childhood friend Rowena, visiting from France, had joined the group for fun and an extremely distressed spirit haunted Clarrie day and night, pressing her to pass on a message, long before Rowena knew for certain that her husband was cheating on her, leading a double life.

Aware of her circumstances, Clarrie had known the advice would be unwelcome, and might be upsetting, so she tried to ignore the persistent spirit. Her mother advised her to pass the message on, because not only was Rowena one of the few people who knew about Clarrie's (often unwanted) gift, but because the ghostly man would give Clarrie no peace until she did.

It transpired that for the previous twenty months, Rowena had suspected Brian of being unfaithful but hadn't wanted to accept that he could be so despicably cunning. His birthday cards to her still expressed his undying love for her and she'd wanted to believe it.

Sarah often encountered such obstinacy. Loved ones who had passed on, still worried about the living and could not be ignored. Clarrie had assumed she knew everything about Rowena's family, her teenage qualms, early marriage and her first son, born a year later, but had no idea who the man could be. However, she'd found out when Rowena delivered some shopping for her.

Over a cup of tea, Rowena was also perplexed until Clarrie delivered his message. *"Tell her she must go to Brian at once, to save him from himself,"* the old man pleaded.

"Did you say he was old, short and quite rotund?" Rowena asked, at first looking puzzled. Then she laughed: "Brian's grandfather, without a doubt. Next time you see him, ask him why I should give up my hopes and dreams for the future, to stick around and mother his worthless grandson!"

It was obvious to Clarrie that, by then, Rowena was quite sure about Brian's infidelity. Now, a couple of years later, she was still in the middle of her unsettled divorce and was currently back in England, staying with an aunt, until her divorce went through and she could return to France.

Rowena's marriage had been fine for nearly thirty years – or so she'd believed. They had been disappointed that, as an RAF officer, he'd seldom served abroad but they had enjoyed the tropical sunshine several times, when visiting Rowena's parents in exotic places. He, especially, appeared to be looking forward to retirement in the south of France because he loved walking and swimming and had already joined a local Gym.

They had a property in the UK, but it was tenanted on a long lease, so they had planned to stay with Rowena's mother, now widowed, while seeking a suitable property to buy, nearer to Languedoc. When the time came, they moved from Scotland to their temporary home in France and Brian encouraged Rowena to start her own company, fulfilling a long-held dream.

He had planned to accept consultancy work, so he could work from his computer at home if he felt like it, but thought his pension would be enough to support them both. With hindsight, after Brian came back from his end of service resettlement course, it was easy to see why Brian had suddenly became restless and said he needed to work in the UK.

Although he had a highly-paid, attractive position on offer locally, he claimed that it didn't appeal to him and Rowena was staggered when he suddenly accepted work in England even though, by doing so, he had deprived their younger son of his free university place. Having a parent at a UK address had saddled him with a huge student loan.

Brian, as usual, had put himself first. Worse, shortly after he started work in the UK, he changed jobs for one paying considerably less money, claiming that it was, "more interesting and better located".

During the following two years, Rowena had tried to visit Brian where he lodged but, at his insistence, they always met halfway – for weekends in London or Brussels. Even contacting him was difficult, as he switched his mobile phone off after six in the evening, every night and when at work used only the office phone.

It eventually became obvious why he had never supplied her, or anyone else in his family, with his real address or a landline telephone number – his 'landlady' was his mistress who lived only a few miles from their own property, which he kept tenanted and therefore unavailable for Rowena to visit, even to decide which of their possessions was to be shipped to France and which could be sold.

Rowena, now, could hardly credit the extent of his deceit and would never contemplate having him back. She pointed out that his grandfather was likely to have been much more concerned about Brian's happiness than hers and, in her words, he should butt-out! "Actually," Rowena added, "I feel quite sorry for the woman Brian's with. He lied to her too, whenever we were together; claiming he was with his son. If she ever finds out how many long weekends we enjoyed, she'll ditch him. He won't be happy for long!"

"You're obviously not at all bitter then," Clarrie had commented, with a wry smile. It was clear that having survived the initial betrayal, she was looking forward to being free and in full control of her life.

Her thoughts were interrupted by the shrill ring of the telephone and, as often happened when she started thinking about someone, at the other end was the subject of her reminiscences, Rowena. "Just when I thought Brian couldn't sink any lower," a very angry Rowena shouted, "he is now refusing to pay back his share of the money my mother lent us, just after my father died."

Clarrie remembered that Brian's plan had been to split their house into two – each with three bedrooms. One would be much larger and include the garden, so could easily be sold. The smaller one they might keep, but this meant a makeover had to be done and they needed a loan. Borrowing within the family was easier than from a bank, but all that was a few years before the marriage broke down and Rowena's mother had not hesitated to help them out, to the tune of £50,000.

They had paid some back but apparently, a few years later, Brian had stopped paying interest on the rest, claiming that it was nothing to do with him – it had been a *gift* to Rowena! No wonder Rowena was wondering what she had ever seen in him! Thank heaven, their sons were both wonderful and a great consolation to her. After calming down, Rowena remarked how glad she was that she had not hurtled back to *save Brian from himself*, as his grandfather had urged.

After she had calmed down and exhausted all the latest news about the divorce, solicitors, *he said, she said* and how long everything was taking, it was clear that as well as being frustrated, she was finding life in the UK a bit dull, compared with her life in France.

Rowena went back to the topic of ghostly interventions commenting that it was the first time

Clarrie had ever given her a direct message from the grave, *or whatever she liked to call it!* "But, now that the subject has come up, there is something I would like to ask." At Clarrie's acquiescent murmur, she continued.

"When we were kids, my parents took us both to visit an old, timbered, house near Worcester. It was reputed to be haunted. You were as thrilled as I was about the books on black magic found in the attic and the human bones dug up from the garden but when you saw it you changed your mind. You insisted on staying in the car – so were you psychic then? Did you see ghosts there?"

Clarrie remembered it vividly. In the ice-cold grip of fear, she'd refused to go anywhere near the old property but, although the atmosphere around it was scary, she confessed that she had not seen anything untoward. Until a few years ago, she had rejected the idea that she might take after her mother, but now that Rowena suggested going there again, she agreed; it would be interesting to see if it still felt the same. Rowena wondered if perhaps Sarah would join them.

Why not, Clarrie considered, after Rowena rang off. Visiting haunted sites with her mother would be fascinating – what amazing things they might discover – but she realised there was no point in suggesting it because, deep down, she knew that her mother never pursued those in the afterlife, preferring to keep a low profile in both worlds!

5. Gavin and Dave

Dave was soon at ease and, naturally enough, was curious to find out what Sarah had experienced that was similar to his son's house being haunted. Gavin glanced apologetically at Sarah – he had not wanted to tell Dave the truth but need not have worried. Sarah said people often blamed mischievous spirits when missing objects reappeared mysteriously. Most were joking, but she knew of at least one haunting, which was not at all funny, so she would listen to his account with an open mind.

Apparently, the young couple had selected the house before the building was completed and were thrilled to have been able to choose some of the fixtures and fittings. The children had settled in quickly, enjoying the garden and having more space in their rooms to play. Although Amy and Holly shared the larger one of the two, Andy felt quite superior having one to himself; on the plans, it was described as an adjoining dressing room. He kept it amazingly tidy as if to demonstrate that he had not been responsible for their messy playroom before the move.

"My son Pete and his wife, Peggy, are not fanciful types," Dave said, "and at first they just supposed that the kids were playing games. On the day they moved in,

Peg thanked the children for collecting and washing up all the coffee cups. Andy, eager to rush away to explore, looked back and said that the Kitchen Lady had done it. Being busy, Peg didn't follow up his flippant remark – it sounded like a joke anyway. It wasn't until other odd things happened, and the children exchanged puzzled glances when censured, that she began to worry."

Dave related the incident they had already heard from Gavin. He and Peg were astonished when the child's toy was found on a high shelf in the airing cupboard, which even he could only just reach. "Could your son, or one of the little girls, have thrown it up there?" Polly asked. Dave said they had thought of that, but it was so carefully placed that it seemed unlikely. The three children spoke of the Kitchen Lady naturally – taking it for granted that their parents were aware of her presence. Polly acknowledged that it must have been disturbing but was eager to hear why they were now even more uneasy about the apparent haunting. Had something bad happened?

"Well," Dave shook his head, "nothing really bad, but if anyone with a weak heart sees what Pete and I have seen, it could be serious."

He spoke quietly, sticking to the facts, obviously trying not to sensationalise. "Every evening, about half an hour after the kids go to bed, Peg goes up to check that all is in order and lights are out but, when Pete took over one night, he heard the rumbling sound of an animal growling. Halfway up the stairs, he froze. When he decided he'd imagined it, he went on to the landing." With a shudder, Dave paused and quaffed a few mouthfuls of beer. "I'd have had trouble believing what happened to him next if it hadn't happened to me too." His account of what occurred had them all agog.

The growling was not imagined – a huge dog was crouched, teeth bared, ready to spring. Snarling, it began to creep forward, out of the darkness, until Pete, terrified, started to back away. It was between him and the door to Andy's room and, at the time, thinking it was real, he decided to step back slowly, hoping it would follow until he could tempt it out of the house, or shout to tell Peggy to ring someone for help.

The creature started to follow but suddenly sprang at him. Had he not been clutching the banister he would have fallen down the stairs... When he recovered his balance, he was alone. He had felt nothing, although the dog could not have avoided landing on his chest, knocking him over.

Polly, who had fallen happily into the role of chief interrogator, asked if he had told his wife. He said he had, of course. She'd never seen or heard anything amiss and insisted on continuing to check on the children personally. Knowing it was a ghost, unable to harm her, was important. She said she would like to assume that it was guarding the children, so he must do the same. The idea of moving to another home was unthinkable and unaffordable, so she was determined to stay. She believed that haunted houses could be exorcised and refused even to discuss selling.

They concluded, after careful probing, that the children were unaware of the dog. The fact that it never appeared to Peg, but had made its presence felt to Pete, struck them as strange. Even when he did not see or hear it, he knew it was there. The air felt icy-cold despite being warm only a few feet away.

When Dave was baby-sitting, although he'd heard about the ghostly dog, he had never expected to see it; apparitions were something other people saw or imagined. As soon as he reached the top of the stairs, he saw it at the far end of the landing, outside the girls' room. There had been no warning snarl or growl. It was difficult, he said, not to turn and run, but he kept reminding himself that it wasn't real and couldn't hurt him if he didn't panic.

"It was grey," he told them, "and huge. It edged towards me with its head down – then it snarled, baring its teeth. I steeled myself to step towards it and it sprang at me. I was scared stiff I can tell you, and it was minutes before I dared move and check on the kids. I hesitated before opening their bedroom doors, as if the thing might appear again and get into the rooms. How stupid can you get!" he added dryly.

"I can understand why you are all so worried," Sarah said, "and impressed by your attitude. I'm sure you are right in thinking that ghosts, however frightening, can't inflict bodily harm. Causing people to panic and injure themselves is another matter." She was satisfied that the account tallied with what she had seen herself and commented that Peg's guess that the dog was guarding the children could be right. "In which case, it would seem that only men are regarded as the enemy. That might be significant."

The history of the area was unknown to Dave; the

site of the estate had been open fields for as long as he could remember. Before they left, Sarah asked if she could visit the house before they went ahead with any exorcism. She said that, before the ghosts were banished, she would dearly like to investigate a little for her own satisfaction; she thought there was a reason for everything.

When Dave looked puzzled, Sarah explained that she was very sensitive to atmosphere and might find similarities with other cases she had known. Gavin nodded in confirmation, and Dave immediately agreed to his suggestion that next time they needed a baby-sitter they should ask Sarah and Polly round. The house would be quiet – unless the kids woke up!

Sarah and Polly exchanged satisfied smiles ...they would look forward to it, they promised.

6. Chasing the Facts

Polly spent an interesting morning at the library and, in the afternoon, with the estate agent who handled the land-sale twenty years ago. The records provided the names of the original owner and first buyer, whose intention was to build a dream property. For some reason, it didn't happen; the agent had no idea why.

Talking it over later with Sarah, who suggested that he might not have been able to get planning permission to build if the land were agricultural, Polly shook her head; it had since changed hands and been built on. Everything pointed to the fact that there must have been a dwelling of some sort on it, which the first buyer intended to replace.

Polly had listed all names relevant to the changes of ownership including that of the speculator, who eventually bought the land to build the estate. When she called on him, as he lived locally, he kindly photocopied plans of the land, before and after the estate was built. The property had been on the market for almost four years after Arthur Simpson left the area, even though Elvis Perry's family were under notice to vacate the remaining cottage. Within a few weeks Arthur would have been able to go ahead with his rebuilding ...so what had made him change his mind?

Who would know?

They could see from the plans that the new estate covered the ground once occupied by the cottages. They must discover more about the situation before babysitting; they needed to be better equipped to understand why at least one house was haunted.

If ghosts were plaguing any other occupants on the site, would they have gossiped about it? More likely, they would have kept quiet, sold up and moved on. Sarah said she would find out how many houses had changed hands and, if possible, contact the original buyers. Polly immediately volunteered to cover that chore... "Oh, I'll be happy to do that. I would be driving you anyway, so if I go alone, it will leave you free to get on with something else."

"What a good idea," Sarah agreed; I can discover most of what we need to know about the history of the site by 'phone." She hoped the ghostly woman and the dog were connected, unsure how she could communicate with a lone animal, especially if it leapt for her throat!... No, she must not be fanciful – only the men had a problem with it. Polly's two granddaughters had never seen or heard anything unusual, but it was unlikely that Gavin would allow either of them to babysit there again.

Within days, they had compiled an impressively thick folder of information, which they could pore over together, away from their computers. Their individual findings had been emailed to each other and carefully printed out, to make discussion easier. Automatically dated emails were useful and easy to keep track of and file, but they preferred talking face to face.

The Jones family occupied the farmhouse long after it ceased to operate as a business and the remaining labourers had been permitted to continue occupying their tied cottages on condition that they maintained them, at their own expense. Eventually, all but one of the three terraced workers' homes fell derelict. When the forty-hectare property finally changed hands, the buyer renovated the farmhouse but allowed the last remaining tenant to stay under the same terms, for only one more year.

His plan was to design and build his dream home – the farmhouse would be a guesthouse. "He probably couldn't get planning permission to build so much on agricultural land," said Polly. "How big is forty hectares anyway? What happened to acres?"

"I think a hectare is just less than two and a half acres and the developer who built the estate had to work hard, years later, to get planning approval – after the village was bypassed, I admit. Even so, what caused the previous owner to change his mind? Nobody gives up on a dream without a fight and I've sensed reluctance on all sides to talk about him," Sarah told her. They were both even keener now, to learn more about the occupants and owners of the site after it ceased to be a working farm. Their next step was to search local newspapers for anything unusual that might shed light on the years in question, between 1982 and 1985. The obvious things could be found on the internet, by setting up a search linked to the locality and the relevant years, so Sarah opted for that task. Polly would spend her time at the library again, surer now of where to look.

Sarah suggested that Dave and his son should visit a few bars to chat to the locals, introducing the subject of ghosts and haunting – without mentioning their own problem, of course. Folk were always eager to talk about anything unusual and it could do no harm, so was worth trying. In that vein, they now had a list of people who had sold estate houses and moved on.

Whilst the Data Protection Act meant they were not supposed to share addresses and personal details, most of the property agents had willingly offered to forward mail when Polly hinted that they were planning a reunion. One or two had just given her the names and addresses they held without much encouragement, which Polly felt was slightly questionable, although it speeded up her research and she was grateful.

Within a couple of days, Gavin reported that he, Dave and Pete had been delighted to have an excuse to pub crawl. There was nothing definite to report, but several people had said, jokingly, that it might account for the Browns' moving out ...one minute they were settled and happy and the next, gone! He promised, laughing, that they would be happy to continue doing the 'rounds', until further notice.

Unwilling to risk the wrath of her daughter, Polly told him to consider the job done. The name, Brown, was already on her new address list; things were going well. She wondered how much longer it would be before they had to babysit but would not admit to being the slightest bit scared ...she preferred to think of it as a frisson of excitement!

Polly's research into significant local events between 1982 and 1985 revealed several interesting facts. She had no idea if any would prove relevant, but they were worth noting. In 1982, a nine-year-old boy had been missing for a week before his satchel was found near the river, as if he had left it there to paddle or it had been washed ashore. His parents said it was extremely unlikely that he would have willingly gone into the water, but something had happened during his twenty-minute walk home from school, which resulted in his disappearance.

The weather had been pleasant earlier that afternoon and, possibly, he was tempted to take a short cut, along the riverbank. Unfortunately, the heavens suddenly opened, and a deluge of heavy rain carried part of the bank into the river. Because his schoolbag was found close to the subsidence, trapped in broken branches and weeds, it was assumed that the boy had fallen in and been swept away.

Later that same year, another boy disappeared from home, but he was a fostered child and had left a note saying he was going home. Polly could find no further reference to him. There were robberies, assaults, burglaries and traffic accidents plus two accidental deaths, but Polly felt her stomach tighten when she read that, within weeks of the presumed drowning, three children were abducted from a cottage on the farm and their mother left for dead. They were never found.

Their father, returning after a night out with a friend, who had given him a lift, found his wife almost battered to death. The friend had been interviewed and he was named in the local press, so Polly made a note of it. If he still lived locally, she would certainly have to talk to him. There was one point, in particular, that caused a quick intake of breath ...*the dog was chained up*. Why?

Sarah had suggested that it would be interesting and might be useful to discover more about the man who was the first buyer of the farm, Arthur Simpson.

As far as Polly could discover, from several people who remembered him, he had lived a quiet life and employed a married couple to run the house, cook and care for him. The husband sometimes walked across the fields to the village to pick up a newspaper – to exercise his legs he said, and he drove his wife out shopping locally, but Mr Simpson was seldom seen. When the farm was offered for sale again, Simpson moved away, leaving the couple in charge until it changed hands.

The librarian remembered the housekeeper well, but she never talked about anything other than books. As far as she knew, the woman was as bewildered as most people by the sudden urge to sell. When the property sold to the developer of the estate, they retired and were living about fifteen miles away. She couldn't remember their name, but Polly knew the estate agent probably had it and their address also, so didn't push her to look it up.

Someone in the queue, who had been unashamedly following the conversation, said she had spoken to 'dear Arthur' just a few weeks before he left, and he certainly did not appear to be considering selling up. On the contrary, he was excited about the architect's plans for extending his house. He had still hoped to get planning permission for a separate, larger place where the cottages stood but, in the meantime, improvements to the original dwelling had been approved.

In case it was needed later, Polly noted carefully the woman's name and telephone number.

He hardly ever came back to this place ...never had, in fact, until a few years ago when his wife's sister, Shirley, married and moved onto the new estate. None of his old friends recognised him; no doubt a full beard and moustache helped! To his wife and her family, he was Elvie, as she hated his first name, so enjoying a pint in *The Grocer's Arms* with his brother-in-law hadn't cause a stir. It was a relief – he wanted no reminders of past times.

Things might have stayed that way had he not volunteered to return some library books for Shirley, who was recovering from a severe hip problem, which was why he and Ellen were here – he would never have come back otherwise. Now, he could scarcely believe his ears – a woman here asking questions, reaping up the past. Why? What possible reason could she have for sticking her nose in!

He would certainly have to watch her – find out more – and, with that in mind, he left ahead of her, determined to watch and follow her until he knew where Ms Nosey Parker could be found, if the need arose.

7. Early Days

Because she still had an hour to spare and now knew more about the situation and the people involved, Polly decided to tackle the most indiscreet estate agent again, luckily, also the one involved in the original estate sale. She could leave her car at the library, as parking would be impossible on the busy street near his agency. It was only a short walk and she needed the exercise, she told herself virtuously!

Harry-the-House as he was known locally, was surprised that she had returned so soon, but happy to stop work for a chat. House sales were slow, he said, and he had nothing urgent to do, so he suggested they went next door for a drink. Next door was a coffee bar, so it was not as decadent as it sounded. As soon as their coffee arrived, Harry started to sip his. "My assistant makes a decent cup, but it never tastes as nice as this, so I bring people in here on the slightest excuse. Now how can I help you?"

"I realise that you were very young when you took over the agency and perhaps have no first-hand knowledge of the farm's history but since I spoke with you," said Polly, "I've discovered several things about the man who bought the farm. You told me he hoped to build a larger modern home on the land and modernise the farmhouse for guests, implying that he had been unable to get planning permission."

"I admit, it was easier to take that line, but I must confess that, at the time, his departure and sudden decision to sell came as a shock – didn't even talk to me about it – just a phone call, followed by confirmation in writing. And, before you ask, the return address was a solicitor in Oxford."

He willingly promised to email it to Polly together with the home address of the couple who had worked for Mr Simpson but didn't think they would be able to tell her anything significant about him. It was obvious that Harry was puzzled by Polly's interest, so she said she was researching local history and wondered if his leaving was influenced by anything that was happening in the village at that time. Harry, having been born in the house where he still lived, was amazed that anyone should find the village interesting enough to care about its past.

Casting his mind back to the nineteen-eighties, he could not remember anything exciting at all. He'd been a typical teenager, he admitted, having little interest in the news, either national or local. When prompted, he did recall a drowning tragedy; the Biggs family lived in his street and Ronald played with his young brother, Kevin. "Funny that! He told us that Ron never stayed with the gang if they went anywhere near water. Who would have thought he'd walk the river path alone?"

"Were the police aware of his fear," asked Polly.

"They must have been told, but if anyone had been with him, they would have raised the alarm when he fell in, wouldn't they? There were search parties out for days, looking everywhere – I even went out with one myself."

Harry knew nothing about the boy who ran away from his foster-parents: didn't even know him. Seeing Polly's disappointment, he took out his mobile and called his brother. After explaining her interest in the village and a lot of silent nodding, Harry asked Polly if she would like to talk to Kev; his car showroom was round the corner and a client had cancelled so he was free. Without hesitation, Polly accepted and was soon sitting comfortably in front of another cup of coffee, in an impressive, modern office.

"You must know that my brother is nicknamed 'Harry-the-House'... They call me 'Kevin-the-Car', did he tell you?"

"No, but you don't seem to mind. I think they sound like marks of affection, or respect, so there's no need for either of you to object, is there?" Kevin nodded his agreement and was eager to be interviewed.

"Are you intending to write a book? Or have you another, more serious reason for asking about the boys I knew as a kid?"

There was no point in lying, but neither was anything to be gained by telling the whole truth, so Polly compromised. She said that she had become intrigued by so many children disappearing within the space of two years when, according to the newspapers, the twenty years before and after had been comparatively uneventful. It seemed like a sensible idea, she said, to look for anything else that, although not world-newsworthy, had happened around the same time, and caused people to be disturbed, or surprised.

Kevin looked puzzled and asked how many children had gone missing. He had clearly forgotten the three from the same family in the farm cottage, until reminded; they were in a younger age-bracket. Anyway, he added, the dogs had been a deterrent to kicking a ball about anywhere near the cottages.

The more Kevin spoke about his childhood, the more enthusiastic he became, and memories flooded back.

Polly threw in odd questions to focus on the points that intrigued her and, by the time she was ready to leave, had a formidable list of notes. They all led to yet more queries but, for now, she knew it was time to stop. Kevin would have talked on, but it was much better to go, promising to let him know if she discovered more.

At the last minute, as if he thought Polly needed encouragement to return, he said, "By the way, it was a mate of my Dad who was with the guy whose wife was left for dead when their kids were abducted. I didn't think of them, when you first asked, because I knew nothing about it when I was little ...not one of my memories! If you like, I can introduce you to Dad. He certainly never believed that the case was properly investigated."

Polly could not have been happier as she drove home.

8. Ghost Hunting

The more she thought about embarking on a ghost hunt the more the idea appealed to Clarrie!

Depending on how much longer Rowena's divorce would take to be finalised, she was sure to like the idea and they need only go on day trips; even with only two eager seekers after truth it would be fun. Del would be away for three weeks, soon, and she had few commitments in his absence, so Rowena could move in. Baby Emma enjoyed car rides and Daxy would be happy wherever she was! He followed her everywhere.

The old haunted house that they had first seen together years ago would be top of their visiting list and Clarrie suddenly had an urge to look for the photographs taken that day. Since they were given to her as a souvenir, she had only looked at them once – when she had shown them to her parents. They were never put into an album – they were still with all the other folders, which she regarded as reference material. Labelled in place and date-order, it was easy to find the half-dozen copied for her by Rowena's father and they were soon spread before her on the table.

Apart from two views of the half-timbered black and white house, most were of the girls with the property in the background but, in several, there was a child she could not recall – noticeable now because she seemed so out of place. A ring at the doorbell called her away to accept a delivery but she returned within minutes, eager to see again the figure she had not noted previously. It was not on any of the snaps. Was she dreaming?

Before she forgot the child's image, Clarrie sketched her, particularly recording her clothing she immediately realised that the little girl was wearing a summer dress. She was certainly oddly out of place but didn't seem to be uncomfortable.

As Clarrie brushed a little watercolour onto the sketch, her eyes strayed again to the photograph ...everyone else in view was more heavily clad; a few people wore woollen caps and scarves. The pictures were taken in February 1975 ...Rowena's father had been very pleased that his new camera had the dating option on it, but her mother thought it ruined the photos, so he reluctantly stopped using it. However, in this case it was confirmation that the weather had been too cold for summer clothing.

Clarrie examined the three photographs in which the child had appeared and sketched plans of them, showing her position in relation to the other sightseers. Another odd fact struck her... In the closest picture, the girl had seemed to be talking to a woman who was leading another child by the hand and ignoring her completely. In a middle-distance shot, the summery-clad girl had been walking away, apparently trailing behind the same woman. Clarrie remembered exactly where the little girl was in the most distant shot of her, but it was not easy to see who would have been near her because there was deeper shadow closer to the building.

Scanning her plans and the photos and saving them into her computer took only a few minutes and she was soon able to blow up the scenes a few hundred per cent. As she suspected, the woman with the little boy was waiting in line to enter the house. Clarrie tried hard to concentrate on her mental picture of the girl, who was obviously out of place... So scantily clad, she would have been the centre of attention had others seen her and the police and Social Services would have been called to the scene; some caring soul would have been talking to her, asking if she were lost!

She was, without doubt, a ghost.

In spite of all the weird and sometimes alarming things she had experienced in the last few years, Clarrie still could not wholly believe in her own psychic ability. Without hesitation, she immediately picked up the 'phone to consult her mother – Sarah would know what to do. As soon as Sarah realised the intriguing nature of the problem, she put the call on 'speaker' so that Polly could hear ...whichever way they handled the matter Polly would be eager to help.

After the call, they downloaded their emails and opened those expected from Clarrie. The attachments were all the photographs she had of that February day, so many years ago. It had occurred to Clarrie that there might be other clues in them that she had missed so she enlarged a few sections of the pictures to pinpoint where the mystery girl had been seen. Clarrie's scans of her own sketches clarified the child's position.

Sarah immediately forwarded them to Alec Holme

with a message. The Detective Chief Superintendent had been a family friend ever since Sarah impressed him many years ago, by redirecting his attention, thus avoiding the embarrassment of a false arrest. Her discretion had resulted in his respecting her desire for privacy and only a small group of officers were aware of her occasional involvement with them.

Alec was at home, recovering from a bout of food poisoning and, now that he felt better, he was at his computer when Sarah's message popped up. Catching up on office work was better than being bored, but when he read the email, all thought of paperwork went from his head. He would never involve his wife in any official case, but there was nothing confidential about this information and she might even be able to help. Jessica sometimes met Sarah socially and would be interested to hear news of her.

Armed with printouts of the message and photographs, Alec found his wife in the kitchen removing a batch of cakes from the oven. "I thought the smell of baking might tempt you from your computer," she said with a wide grin. "You should be resting and recovering your strength, not working." She slapped his outstretched hand as he moved towards the cakes... "For goodness sake, let them cool – you'll have indigestion on top of your other problems, if you don't watch out!"

"I have something to show you," Alec said, waving the sheaf of papers in the air, so I'll lay these out on the dining table. Have you time to look before we eat?"

Jessica was eager to see everything and intrigued to hear that Clarrie, after so many years had elapsed, had seen a child in the photographs. "The little girl must have been present, in spirit, on the day these were taken. Perhaps Clarrie sensed her presence then and knew that something was not right. That's why she didn't want to leave the car."

Jessica was familiar with the old haunted house, having lived within forty miles of it before marrying, and she had retained an interest in local news. There had been many tragic or unfortunate happenings over the years, but she couldn't recall anything specific that might relate to the child described by Clarrie. She did volunteer to help if her knowledge of the area was of use.

Although the investigation could not be official, Alec had already ordered a search through the records of the relevant years for anything that might relate to Clarrie's vision. Whether crime related or not, he knew, from earlier experiences with Sarah and Clarrie, that finding the answer would not be a waste of time.

He didn't hesitate to forward the email to Detective Inspector Algy Green. The DI and his wife had been Clarrie's friends for many years and would be eager to help. Algy could decide, depending how things developed, whether to bring in the detective sergeants who completed the discreet team that had worked with Sarah many times. So close to retirement, Detective Superintendent Holme often felt he was marking time and was frustrated with the daily routine ...this would certainly be more interesting than some of his current in-tray of insurance fraud cases and he looked forward to receiving answers soon, to all that he had set in motion.

9. Seen but Not Heard

After sending the email to her mother, Clarrie tried to catch up with other mail before shutting down her computer but, although she was sure that she had exited her photograph folder, the half-dozen pictures in question were still there on her screen. It was weird, but she became more intrigued and could not bring herself to switch them off again; she would show them to Del later.

The small child in the flowery, summer dress wriggled closer to the monitor, eagerly. She understood less than Clarrie did about what was happening. She did know her name. She was Elly. She kept trying to tell people she was Elly, but nobody listened. She was eight-years-old, a big girl, so she was always proud to look after her baby brother.

Elly tried to remember why he'd stopped talking to her and didn't even seem to see her any more. She wanted to take him home – she could not go home without him – but he'd clutched the hand of a strange lady and ignored all her pleading. Time had stood still for Elly, but little Jamie kept changing and growing until she had to look up at him. Eventually, he changed so much that she scarcely knew him, and Elly was more and more confused. She drifted in and out of a new, strange space. Her only connection to reality had gone.

When Clarrie recalled the old photographs and the day she had visited the timbered house, it was a memory she shared, unknowingly, with Elly, a little girl she had never met. If Rowena's father had pointed his camera in any other direction Clarrie would never have known that Elly was there. Now, gazing at the photographs on the screen, Elly saw only her little brother and the lady... Where was she? Turning to look at Clarrie, Elly was reminded of the girl she had asked for help, but who had turned away and not even followed her friends ...it couldn't be her though, she was much too old.

Watching Clarrie sketching earlier, seeing a picture of herself emerge, in her pretty frock, Elly had been fascinated. It was her favourite dress.

The picture proved that she must have been there, didn't it? She suddenly felt safe; still not understanding, but no longer feeling alone, the child relaxed. Now, surely, she would have help finding Jamie and be able to take him home.

10. A Good Neighbour

Minnie Travis paused to thank her neighbour for offering to help. In her mid-seventies, she still liked to hang out her own laundry and folding the dry, sweet-smelling, fluffy towels was a real pleasure.

Dora Mace, who had lived next door for years, was kind enough, but there was something about the woman that she still found unsettling – she had a habit of stopping mid-sentence to tilt her head, for instance, as if listening to some distant sound. Her handsome young son had been sickly when they moved in and had been such a skinny little toddler – spent most of his time in bed. Dora's husband had deserted them, and she seemed to shrink under the stress of caring for the infant alone.

All her own offers to sit with the boy so that Dora could rest were turned down – she was, after all, a stranger; she understood and was not offended. Then, after weeks of catching only fleeting glimpses of Dora, she saw her taking Joe out in his pushchair. It was such a relief, knowing the child must be getting better.

A few days later, the little boy started playing in the garden and Minnie was delighted to see, from her window, that he had filled out a little and was sturdy enough to kick a ball about but, as soon as she went out to talk to him, Dora swept him up and took him inside...

"Time my little man had his afternoon nap," she said. Minnie loved children and was disappointed, but things gradually changed as Dora became much more confident that Joe was strong enough to make friends.

Minnie became like a grandma to him and missed him as much as his mother did when, grown-up, his job took him away from home for weeks at a time.

Dora rarely thought about the early years. Her memories, when they returned, were selective: Joe white and thin, wasting away, and chubby little Joe miraculously restored to health. They melded into one child playing happily in the garden. She sometimes pondered about the 'Elly' that he kept asking for. Deliberately, she pushed away the vision of the girl she had left behind, who had been trying to steal him from her. Her overriding duty was to take care of Joe, her darling boy.

They must have gone out to enjoy the fresh air that day, to bring some colour to his cheeks. She had been frantic with worry about him for so long – waiting for the doctor to visit Joe again, but day after day passed and he didn't come. He'd said that Joe would have to go into hospital and she was frightened that, when he did come, it would be to take Joe away.

It had been a tremendous relief when the sea breeze performed a miracle and Joe had never looked back. He was clever at school too and was now an officer in the army. He liked to travel but she missed him and was like a lost soul until he returned. Dora was so happy, preparing Joe's room for his weekend at home. It had been at least three months since he last had any leave, during which time it had not been entered. If she went in when he was away, even to dust, she came out feeling depressed.

Humming happily to herself, she threw the bottom sheet over the mattress and tucked it in neatly before moving to do the same on the other side. She shrieked with alarm when her feet sank into the carpet pile with ominous squelching sounds. She looked up in horror and saw the ceiling dark and cracking under the weight of water seeping from the loft. Simultaneously she felt a heavy drip on her arm.

She couldn't remember when she last went up there but knew that the water tank must be leaking...

There was a pole somewhere to open the trapdoor and lower the ladder – but she couldn't even recall where it was! It was bound to be handy – she would find it while waiting for the plumber – but she had no regular plumber – she must ring Minnie, next door, she would know who to contact.

While waiting for Minnie to pick up the 'phone, Dora had a flashback to climbing the ladder, not long after she moved in, and she was carrying a blanket. It had been Joe's favourite: large, soft and covered with pictures – and he couldn't be separated from it when he was ill. She pondered about why Joe had never asked for it after he got better ...then Minnie's voice answered and broke into her thoughts. She promised to telephone a man who she was sure would come immediately and said she was on her way to help if she could, so Dora mustn't worry.

Dora, however, could not stop worrying.

Why did just thinking of the attic make her feel ill?

Why had she taken that beautiful blanket away from Joe?

Why hadn't he missed it?

All these other worries were, at least, preventing her from fretting about the leak and Minnie, when she arrived, was perturbed to find her far from her normal, chatty self.

Minnie couldn't help noticing that Dora seemed distracted and unfocussed ...much like she had been twenty years ago when they first met.

11. Heard but Not Seen

Elly stared, fascinated, at the computer. Clarrie had gone to the kitchen to make sure the evening meal was cooking satisfactorily and had left an image of the woman and small boy on the computer. It was the closest the pair had been to the camera and, adjusted to crop off the background, they filled the screen. Elly could not take her eyes off Jamie...

How did he get here?

He had been walking and moving in a strange house and would not talk or listen to her ...just as if she wasn't there and now he was here, in a box!

It made her want to cry.

Somehow, it seemed a long time since she had seen him... Where had she been? Vague images of unfamiliar places drifted through her mind. Elly was supposed to have been looking after Jamie and, having failed, she was unable to think much beyond her overwhelming guilt.

Lost and lonely, she grieved in a vacuum where time had no meaning. Sometimes, she found herself in what she accepted as Jamie's house, but he was no longer the same. Memories of their own home stayed fresh, but the desire to find it had faded... How could she face Mammy and Daddy after what she had done?

Still fresh in her mind was her repeated failure to make Jamie hold hands and come with her, Elly had drifted away to get help but was lost.

When it happened, they were both with Nana and Gramps, having a *'nice day out to give Mammy a rest'*, Nana said, and the sun was shining.

Everywhere was strange to Elly and she could not even guess which way would lead home. It didn't matter until she realised that Jamie had slipped from her grasp; she was alone ...and she couldn't go home without Jamie anyway.

Her dress, heavy with water wrapped itself tightly around her legs as she had struggled to get to him; the water dragged her back, pulling her down as it filled her nose and mouth.

He had gone away with a stranger. He knew he should not talk to strangers ...*bad boy!*

Her determination to reach Jamie overcame her terror and she was relieved suddenly to find herself warm and dry, following the stranger who was still in sight, taking her little brother away in a chair with wheels.

All she could do was trail behind them, until she saw that Jamie, looking a little better, was helping to push the chair.

Anxiety must have lent wings to her feet because she was soon clutching at Jamie's hand, trying to pull him away. Frightened when he didn't respond, she began to worry about where Nana and Gramps were but didn't dare to leave him to look for them, for fear of losing him too.

Eventually the strange lady carried him onto a bus. Jamie was excited, because he usually only travelled by car.

Elly watched as he relaxed more and more with the stranger. She was kind to him and pointed out boats on a river and animals in a field. She made animal noises, which he imitated with glee. It was a long ride and the bus kept stopping for people to get on and off.

When they eventually got off the bus they walked to a house in the middle of a row with a small garden in front.

Since that day, Elly had rarely left that house.

Her thoughts often turned to her own home, but she lacked the incentive to find it. How could she be forgiven for losing her little brother?

Now, staring at the computer screen, Elly's mind whirled. *How had she come to be in this new place? Where was she? Who was the strange lady and why did she have pictures of Jamie with that dreadful person? This was her baby brother as he really was ...not at all like the one who was in his place. What had happened since she last saw him; perhaps he had changed back?* When Clarrie walked in and shut down the computer Elly shrieked to stop her.

Clarrie whirled in astonishment. She saw no one and heard nothing more, but she did restore the pictures. As before, she had no option but to ring her mother.

Listening in awe, between her wails of distress, Elly was thrilled; *she had been heard.* Nothing now would tempt her to leave Clarrie and the magic box.

Polly listened open-mouthed and could only guess what Clarrie was saying in answer to Sarah's questions.

She knew that Sarah would tell her when the call was over, so she hurried off to the kitchen to make coffee. They had eaten already and were just about to watch the news on TV.

Earlier, she had been eager to go through her notes with Sarah. She had amassed a formidable quantity of loose papers and needed to know which leads to follow.

She was particularly pleased with the information she had dragged out of Kevin-the-Car and he had given her his father's telephone number so that she could arrange to meet him soon. As a first approach, Polly felt it would be far better to speak to him rather than email. If he were still in contact with the bereaved husband, it would be fantastic.

Now she was torn between wanting to give her own news and hearing Clarrie's.

Television was forgotten when Polly re-joined Sarah as her call ended, and she learned that the ghostly child was now haunting Clarrie. "Do you think it possible that I too would hear her, being clairaudient?" she asked hopefully.

"Well, how soon would you like to find out?" Sarah smiled. "We could go tomorrow and, depending on how things turn out, we can either come straight back or stay overnight. It rather depends on how your research is going. I think our priority has to be Dave's ghostly dog."

It was a signal for Polly to take over and present her findings.

She had always been well-organised and had already whittled her folders down to three:

Past Events.

Several children disappeared prior to the three from the *cottage where mother was left for dead and *guard-dog was chained.

Simpson's sudden decision to sell the farm and land?

Current Plan

To be interviewed —

1. The couple who looked after Arthur Simpson, the farm's owner.
2. Mr and Mrs Brown who unexpectedly sold their estate house and moved on.
3. Kevin-the-Car's Dad who knew Elvis Perry, the bereaved father, and the man who was with him when he found his wife, beaten.

The Haunting

*Ghostly dog — Why does it only appear to men?

As Polly relayed all she could recall of her interviews, she tucked her scribbled notes into the relevant folders and Sarah agreed with her about following up her three selected leads.

There had been less luck in tracing Arthur Simpson. Little was known about him or where he'd lived previously, and he had not made any close friends in the area.

In comparison to all the information that Polly had gathered, Sarah declared herself a complete failure!

"And, of course," Sarah pointed out, "you now have to add another folder to your collection – we have Clarrie's little friend to worry about. I might have more luck in communicating with a child, rather than a dog!"

It was clear that their time would be better spent helping Clarrie for a day at least, so they decided to have an early night and drive over to see her at crack of dawn. Knowing that Clarrie needed their help, it was difficult to concentrate on anything else anyway.

They would be in a better position to help Dave if they had nothing else on their minds.

12. Ways Less Frightening

Del had always been a good listener and Clarrie was eager to tell him about the unseen presence in their house. She knew he would be more interested in discovering the reason for the child's sudden arrival than nervous about her being a ghost.

After years of reporting from abroad he was now involved in researching 'cold' cases, liaising with the CID, and was ideally placed to help, if only she could discover enough clues from the little girl about where to begin. She contained herself until dinner was over and they were enjoying coffee in the sitting room before announcing, "My mother and Polly are coming tomorrow – probably only for the day."

As expected, his first reaction was to ask why they were not staying overnight... "I won't see anything of them if they drive straight back. What's their rush to go home?"

Of course, she knew little about the case they were looking into for Dave – they might tell her more about that tomorrow, but she explained to Del all that had happened to her today and why she needed Sarah's help.

He examined all the photographs and intuitively went straight to the reason for the child's presence. "Although you didn't see her when the photos were taken, she must have noticed you – probably because you were nearer to her own age than the grown-ups. You say she seemed to be looking at you in one of the snaps – so she might even have spoken to you. Even that small connection might have created a link that brought her to you when you re-examined the photos and momentarily saw her in them."

Clarrie could think of no better explanation and was glad he had put into words exactly what she had imagined. She promised to ring him if Sarah and Polly could not sleep over, so that he could come home in time to see them.

They had an early night after watching a film on TV and Clarrie could not sleep immediately. She should perhaps have included Rowena in the email she had sent to her mother... Rowena would be fascinated if such psychic ability as she possessed were more like her mother's. It would, in this case, have been more useful but, on the other hand, it would have interfered more with her normal life. Revelations came to her in ways less direct, and altogether less frightening, for which she was thankful. Such were her thoughts as she drifted off.

Her sleep was at first dreamless...

Then Clarrie became aware that the sun was shining, and she watched as an elderly couple strolled along a grassy bank. There was water below; lake or sea – or perhaps a river, she was unsure ...it was moving and frothy. Two children ran ahead to look down, causing the couple to panic – the man ran after them, shouting for them to stop and wait.

As the little girl turned, Clarrie recognised her as

the child in the photographs. The small boy broke free of her grip and ran on. Startled and, aware now of danger, the girl ran to stop him. As she grabbed his arm he stumbled and they both disappeared over the edge.

Clarrie's fright was so great that she woke immediately and lay shaking. Concentrating on what she had seen, she gradually relaxed and tried to sleep again. Gradually, she caught glimpses of the little boy and seemed to be falling with him... She was holding his arm – no – not his arm, his sleeve – then just his coat – and she was in the water and saw him a few yards away.

She tried to reach him, but an undertow was pulling her down. The water carried them both ...on ...and on. Frantic now, fighting for breath, she saw that the high bank had gone and a woman at the water's edge was lifting a child onto dry land; it was her brother. Crying aloud with relief she struggled nearer to them and held out her arms to be rescued too, but the woman turned away with Jamie in her arms.

Clarrie, wide-awake again, was so wet with perspiration that she really did feel as if she'd been swimming. She knew now how the girl had died – it was horrible. Knowing that she could have been saved was sickening; how could anyone have abandoned her so callously? She knew even more, which could be helpful in tracing the girl's identity... Her brother had survived, and his name was Jamie.

The remainder of the night passed undisturbed and on the following day Sarah and Polly arrived, in plenty of time for coffee, eager to hear at first hand all that Clarrie could tell them about her resident ghost.

13. Ghost Stories

Several nights ago, in his local, *The Grocer's Arms*, Theo Penn had overheard a few ghost stories, which all the tellers swore were true. The chap who started it did not claim to have seen one himself, but Theo suspected he had – otherwise, why would he have brought up the subject?

It had been on the tip of his tongue to join in. For fifty years, until he retired, he had been a caretaker and night-watchman at Grennish Place, the local old-folk home. In the old days, it had been an asylum for unfortunate people sick in the head and he reckoned he'd seen quite a few of their ghosts.

His own granddad had been one of the ill-fated patients there and Theo was sure his spirit often sat with him when he was on duty. The old man had died before Theo grew old enough to know him, but it was weird and wonderful to imagine that his granddad knew him and wanted to be with him. Theo told nobody about the poor, lost souls he saw. Some saw him watching them, but he never heard them speak. Others drifted aimlessly, not meeting his eye.

If, at the pub, he had joined in the general repartee, he would have told them about the woman he knew before and after her death.

He hadn't known her well but had collected her boy from school, after sports, a few times as a favour and sometimes saw her working around her cottage when he walked his dog. He had rarely approached too near, being cagey about the huge guard dogs. Although he had seen how playful they were with the children, they might be fierce with strangers.

What a sad end for such a nice family ...the children abducted, and their mother beaten almost to death.

She ended up in Grennish Place because she never recovered her sanity or memory. Before she died, she wandered the grounds tearfully, looking for her children, not capable of understanding what had happened to them, or her. Theo didn't understand either, but he kept a friendly eye on her, making sure she always returned safely to her ward.

For many years, after she died, she appeared to him almost every night. It was as if she still lived in the building but now came and went as she wished. He believed that she went out to the cottage, which had been her home, still searching for her children ... unsuccessfully, apparently, as she always returned in tears.

Funnily enough, around the time he and his wife moved into their new house on the estate, the ghostly woman stopped appearing to him; she must have given up and moved on, to wherever the dead are supposed to go.

He wished now that he *had* told his story in the pub. Someone might have heard whether her kids were ever found. He hoped they were.

Gazing from his bedroom window, Theo could see down the whole length of the avenue and wondered, again, where exactly the labourers' cottages had been; it was difficult to recall the open fields and woodland as he had known them in his youth. So much time had gone by and so many things had changed and, sadly, there were many questions that might never be answered.

14. Questions

Having told Clarrie about their own ghostly mystery, Sarah was anxious to hear everything else she had discovered about the child in the photos. Of course, the impression they had now formed of the circumstances surrounding the child's death saddened them all and made them even more anxious to discover the reason for her being tied to the earthly plane, rather than accepting that she had passed on.

Since entering the house, Sarah had been aware of an unearthly presence, but did not sense any attempt being made to contact her. She guessed that the child was keeping close to Clarrie, in whom she probably had complete faith. It was easy to guess that seeing her brother Jamie, with Clarrie's help, she now expected more of her... It was clear that she wanted to be reunited with him, not realising that now, most likely, he was a man and what she hoped for was impossible.

Clarrie said that she had already let Alec know that he should be looking for reports involving two children – one being a boy named Jamie, probably James, a toddler. Every time his name was repeated, Sarah's stomach tightened, and she knew she was sharing this sensation with the child. Staring into every corner of the room for a few minutes, she watched the afternoon sun filter through the curtains, lighting the stone fireplace in a warm glow. She allowed her eyes to wander over the framed oil painting above it and the walls at each side lined with shelves of books, trying to empty her mind of everything except the two children. As she had hoped, picturing Jamie hand in hand with the woman in the photograph, the image of a little girl came into focus. She risked speaking aloud. "Hello, I'm Sarah. Please tell me your name. Why are you here? Can we help you?"

Polly and Clarrie stopped talking, suddenly realising what Sarah was doing.

Sarah did not speak aloud again but they remained quiet and waited patiently until she opened her eyes and sat back with a deep sigh. "All I gained from seeing our little ghost was confirmation of what we already guessed. She was so excited to be heard that she didn't answer any of my questions. She just kept telling me that she must find Jamie and she can't go home without him. He's not where he is supposed to be. I promised to help if she tries hard to describe where they used to live and where she thinks he should be now." Although nothing new and significant had transpired, it was encouraging that Sarah was now in contact with the child.

Del was delighted that their visitors were able to stay overnight and made copious notes about both hauntings, so that he could search his newspaper archives. Polly and Del cleared up together after supper, allowing Sarah and Clarrie to have some private time together, then they all tried to relax but it was impossible to stop speculating about why the ghostly hound didn't like men or how long ago the child had drowned while trying to save her brother. It was a fair guess that, as the little boy in the photographs was recognisable to Clarrie as the boy in her dream, the drowning must have been over twenty years ago. As for the dog – Del suggested that, in life, a man had ill-treated either him or the children he loved. There must be something, he said, that connected the living children to those the dog had known. There was no way of knowing how long ago that was.

Polly repeated eagerly what she'd heard about the three children who were abducted from the cottages that had once stood somewhere on the land occupied now by the estate. When she repeated what she had been told about the dog being chained up, all but Sarah were ecstatic – convinced that there was a connection.

Sarah, as always, advised caution. "We mustn't jump to conclusions, although I admit it is worth considering and following up. Anyway, well done Polly, you have discovered a lot in such a short time." Looking through Polly's notes, she commented, "I see that you plan next to visit the people who moved unexpectedly, soon after buying their estate house. The address you have here is not far off our route home, so why don't you ring up and see if we could drop in tomorrow?"

Without giving the real reason for their requesting a meeting, Polly called the number given by the estate agent, hoping they had not moved again, and obtained permission to visit Enid and Edward Brown any time after lunch.

Clarrie was eager to revisit the old house where the photographs had been taken but didn't even try to persuade Sarah to come with her and Rowena. Hoping to encourage their little ghost to make contact with Sarah, Clarrie loaded the photographs onto her laptop and left it open on a side table. They were on a loop and each picture showed for ten seconds.

Conversation flowed seamlessly from one subject to another, but Sarah listened more than she joined in. She was aware that the child was present and totally gripped by the images of the woman with the toddler who was, apparently, her brother.

Sarah concentrated and, mentally, asked a question; *"Is that your brother Jamie?"*

Her little face alight with hope, the girl turned to Sarah and asked a string of questions of her own. She wanted to know why the lady had taken him away and why Jamie wouldn't talk to her ...and where Jamie went because he's not there anymore ...and finally, bursting into tears, she asked if Sarah would tell her mommy and daddy that losing Jamie wasn't her fault.

Sarah promised to try but said she would need lots of help to find them. Most importantly, she needed to know their names and all about the place where they lived.

Soon, the others became aware that Sarah was not taking part in their chat and that she was writing on the back of Polly's notes with half-closed eyes. They continued to talk, but they were now much more interested in what they might hear from Sarah when she saw fit to speak to them!

15. Calling for Answers

Enid Brown was perturbed. When Ed asked her why their visitors wanted to call on them, she realised that she didn't really know. "For goodness sake! Surely you asked," he demanded, irritated because his quiet afternoon would be disrupted. "What did the woman actually say? She's probably selling religion or double-glazing."

"She really didn't sound like a salesperson," Enid protested, more than a little fed-up with Edward's antisocial attitude. While he was glued to the TV, every afternoon, she wrote letters or cut recipes from old magazines; having visitors would be a nice change.

Since moving into their new house – their second new house inside two years – Enid had not been at all happy. It was Ed who had insisted on leaving the estate, where she had just begun to make friends. She blamed Theo Penn. One of his stupid stories, or something he had told Ed had thoroughly upset him – scared him even – and her husband put their house on the market without even talking it over with her.

He had eventually admitted that, from other things the old man had said, Ed really believed that Mr Penn, their neighbour, was psychic and couldn't ignore his warning, that...

The chime of the doorbell interrupted her thoughts and Enid hastened to meet her callers.

Polly first established that it was she who had telephoned, and then introduced Sarah. Enid looked flustered and was, in fact, very nervous after what Ed had said. What had she been thinking of, inviting two strangers to visit them? ...What could they possibly need to speak about?

She was reassured slightly when Ed rose to greet their guests with a pleasant smile, seated them comfortably and offered them a drink of wine or fruit juice – or anything.

Nobody would have believed how much he resented the intrusion!

Conversation flowed easily after Polly explained that they had friends living on the estate, not far from the house she and her husband had recently left, and Ed relaxed even more when he recognised the name, Peter Fletcher. "Pete used to come into my local sometimes with his father, Dave," Ed said. "Fine darts players – both of them."

It was difficult to explain the reason for their intrusion without being frank and Sarah felt there was nothing to be lost by asking if the reason for their moving away had been anything to do with the location of the house.

Enid immediately said she had loved everything about the place and she looked pointedly at her husband. "It was Edward who was unhappy there – ever since that crazy man warned him that it was doomed."

Ed was obviously annoyed with Enid for revealing his weakness, in taking any notice. Ed had ignored Theo initially, even though everyone said the man was psychic, but when the old man grew agitated and persisted – and reminded him of personal things he had himself almost forgotten – Ed was shaken. Rolling a car over and ending upside down in a ditch was something he had never even told Enid... He had been driving, under age, and his older brother took the blame! Only the two of them knew the truth and his brother had died years ago. After that, how could he not take the warning seriously?

Ed said he felt bad for the people buying the house but what else could he do? He and Enid were not wealthy enough to abandon it and buy another; it was a matter of self-preservation. Theo Penn had predicted that his roof would fall in – come crashing down through the house. He didn't know when it would happen, and Ed defended his silence about the prophecy by saying that there was no reason to think anyone was inside at the time and was injured; he was just being sensible; apart from the inconvenience a new roof would cost a lot. He had the grace to look embarrassed, but Sarah and Polly understood.

There was no reason to be specific about houses being haunted so Sarah tried to discover more about Theo Penn. The Browns didn't know much. Neighbours were a little wary of him because he seemed sometimes to be talking and laughing with 'the invisible man', as one of them put it. Ed explained... "Once, when wished *'Goodnight Theo'* he abruptly stopped talking and did a 'double-take', as if surprised to find himself alone!" Apparently, since then, Theo had kept very much to himself and often ignored people who tried to be friendly, so his company was avoided.

Polly said it is often the case when someone doesn't quite fit in; they become the subject of gossip and speculation. It happens with all age groups and accounts for a lot of bullying in schools.

After Polly and Sarah had gone, Ed asked Enid, "So why did they come then? Surely, we would have heard if anything untoward had happened to the house. They seemed more interested in old Theo."

Enid smiled. She really had no idea why they'd called but was very glad that they had. She had enjoyed meeting them and invited them to visit again whenever they drove to see Sarah's daughter. She and Polly had exchanged recipes and the afternoon had been the most stimulating she could remember for a long while.

16. Theo Finds a Friend

Polly was excited by the thought that there was someone on the estate who might be psychic and living quite close to Pete Fletcher's family – on the same road, in fact. She wondered if they knew Mr Penn and as soon as she could, after settling back at home, she rang Pete to ask.

It seemed that Theo was well known on the estate. He was thought, by some, to be weird because he talked aloud to himself as he walked along, smiling and nodding as if he were not alone, but most people considered him harmless. His near neighbours obviously liked him.

Theo Penn sat on the box seat in the bay window of his bedroom. He stared sadly at the house opposite, and bitterly regretted that he had felt compelled to warn Ed of what he feared would happen if he and Enid did not move out.

His vision had been so clear that morning. He was half-awake, looking forward to what promised to be a sunny day, when he suddenly saw the ceiling above him shatter and fall, and the noise was tremendous... but he knew it was not his ceiling – not his bed – it was Edward Brown's, where he was asleep, with his wife Enid beside him – a detail he did not reveal when he recounted his vision to Ed.

It was not difficult to convince his friend that they were in danger; Ed had received ample proof of Theo's psychic abilities and, although feeling a little guilty, he immediately put their house up for sale. He adopted the rationale that they if they moved out, it would never happen! If it could be avoided, it was for the best.

Theo missed them. He and Ed had the odd pint together and Enid had invited him to Sunday lunch several times. He sighed, recalling her excellent cooking. He was about to turn away from the window when a car drew up outside. There was no doubt that it was someone intent on calling on him, and, sure enough, the passenger door opened, and an unfamiliar woman stepped out. She was smartly dressed and, he guessed younger than he was. She waited for the driver to join her and then they walked into his driveway.

In panic, Theo hurried downstairs to make sure his home was still fit to receive visitors. Although he didn't have many, his front room was always welcoming, with comfortable, leather armchairs and rosewood display cabinets. An embroidered fire screen hid the empty grate and standing beside it a flowering plant gave the room a touch of life.

He was almost fanatical about keeping it tidy but had been sorting through photographs and putting them in his albums during the morning and they were spread all over the Chesterfield. The doorbell rang, and he realised he couldn't move them in haste without muddling them again, so he sighed and went to answer the door; they might not want to come in anyway.

The woman passenger introduced herself and said

that they had recently visited Enid and Edward Brown. She introduced Polly, the heavier-built, older woman and said they had promised to call on him to convey best wishes from his former neighbours. They accepted his immediate invitation to join him for tea and, after making sure they were comfortable, he started trying to move his photographs to a safe place on the window sill – the only surface free of ornament.

Sarah helped him and, on the spur of the moment, asked if he had any old pictures of the farmland, before the estate was built. He pulled a couple of albums from the pile and said that, if he had, they would be in one of them... He really couldn't remember.

While he boiled the kettle for tea, she and Polly eagerly turned the pages and enjoyed searching through the faded snaps, recognising familiar parts of the county, which had changed dramatically over the last half-century, and not always for the better.

The farm cottages appeared on many of the photos, from different directions: sometimes in the distance beyond the focus of interest. None were of any help – although they didn't really know what they were looking for! When the door opened again, and Theo pushed a trolley in, a sudden gust of wind blew through the unsorted piles on the sill and they flew in all directions. Theo hastened to shut the window.

"Goodness me, I do apologise, I had no idea the latch wasn't secure." He was upset and wondered how long he had been vulnerable to any chance burglar! He started to pick up the photos but stopped immediately when Sarah jumped from her seat and darted in front of him. She had recalled a similar incident, many years ago, when Clarrie's collection fell to the floor in disarray and, on top, were the pictures that she had failed to find.

"Please let me pick them up for you. I'll try to sort them a bit while you pour the tea – it would be a pity to let it grow cold.

As she suspected, and had hoped, one picture had landed well apart from any others and it was of Theo's dog enjoying a romp in the fields beyond the workers' cottages. In the back garden of the nearest one, a woman was pegging out clothes while three children played nearby. Having stacked the others tidily, Sarah carried her 'find' to show Polly. Polly stared at it, initially with interest but then in puzzlement. In answer to Sarah's lifted eyebrow she could only shrug and mouth *later*.

Theo still had no idea of their real reason for calling but, once settled, he was eager to talk about his friends. They had written several times, giving him their address and inviting him to visit them but he had never answered. He didn't own a car – had never driven in his life – but he had considered taking a bus. He'd never got around to checking the timetables and, although he didn't mention it, he began to feel guilty about having been responsible for their moving away. Time went by and they stopped writing to him.

If anything were to be gained by talking to Theo, Sarah knew they must be as open as possible with him, so she immediately said that they had friends living on the estate who were probably known to him. He seemed pleased that he did know the young family who lived on the same road as he did, although not well, he added.

When Sarah said that their reason for contacting the Browns was to discover if they had been driven to sell because of any unusual happenings in their house, Theo's smile froze...

Polly came to Sarah's rescue, and told him about possible supernatural disturbances in the young family's home. Sarah, she told him, had a little experience in such things and had been asked to advise them about what they should do. Ed Brown had been unable to help but had suggested that they contact Theo. "So, we wonder if you know of others in the same quandary," she said, "and that is why we are here, unannounced, seeking your help."

Somewhat mollified, Theo relaxed. It was apparent that Ed had not betrayed his confidence. People already thought he was dotty; they didn't need any encouragement.

His ghostly visions had started when he was a child and, not being able to separate them from the living, his reputation for being weird was long-standing. By the time he was old enough to realise what was happening it was too late, but he soon learned how to glance around him when addressed unexpectedly, to make sure that others could see what he could see or were far enough away for it not to matter. This alone made others wary of him, so he never had close friends.

He took his strange talent for granted, never seeking to experiment, or ask for guidance. Ghosts, he'd decided a long time ago, were dead people who couldn't rest. It mattered not one jot to him, whether they came or went, and most people didn't believe they were there anyway!

Fortunately, they didn't appear often and seemed to understand that he was no use to them; if they did communicate with each other, they most likely dismissed him as strange, just as the living did. He was a nonentity in both worlds. His mind had been elsewhere, but he suddenly realised that Sarah was handing him a photograph. "Oh, yes," he said, "I do remember the people who lived there, particularly the woman."

He needed little encouragement to talk about her, having known her before and after her death. "It was a great tragedy. Her children were kidnapped, and she was so badly beaten that she never recovered – lost her mind – and ended up in the mental ward of the hospice."

Sarah and Polly were fascinated to hear that he had been a night-watchman there and that he had often found her wandering the grounds at night, crying, trying to return home to be with her children. Her husband didn't visit her after the first week, Theo told them: "It must have been too distressing, losing the children and his wife not recognising him. He came to her funeral, then I never heard any more of him."

Theo went quiet, his mind drifting to the woman again. Her spirit had wandered back and forth, even when the cottages were flattened, and the estate was being built – then after the houses became occupied she never came back to the hospital. Perhaps he had been too preoccupied moving to the estate himself to notice. As if he had called out for her, the woman appeared before him, in the room with the three of them, and she was smiling.

He sat nonplussed, not daring to look directly at her.

Sarah saw her too, and silently asked her if she had found her children. With a smile and a nod, the woman faded away. Sarah was thrilled. She knew that she would be able to contact the ghostly woman again but was less optimistic about learning anything of value. It was likely that the children she'd claimed as hers were not those who were kidnapped all those years ago.

More to the point, only by convincing the poor mother of her mistake, would she be able to rescue the family from being haunted. The dog had to be connected to the dead woman – he was with her when she was hanging out laundry in the photo.

It gradually dawned on Theo that Sarah had seen the woman too and he was immensely excited. It was such a relief to share his ghosts and Sarah was forced to admit that she had been able to see her – and yes, she did see lost spirits sometimes. Theo assumed that Sarah was as ignorant as he was himself, about why they appeared and why some spoke to him, just as if they were alive. He confessed that he was almost scared of speaking to strangers, in case they weren't really there...

Sarah advised him to ask them silently, in his head, how he could help them. If they were spirits, they would answer the same way, and nobody nearby would know they were there. Theo looked extremely doubtful but promised to try. It was easy then, to explain that the woman he had known was haunting the young family they were trying to help.

Theo saw the logic – their three children were similar in age to her own – but he wondered how he could help, if at all. Once assured that they needed as much information as he could give them about the tragedy of the kidnapping and her family, there was no stopping Theo.

Although he had never regarded the family as anything other than acquaintances, Theo had sometimes helped the woman back to her car with heavy shopping. He had always felt sorry for her having three young children, so close in age. The oldest, the boy, had to be taken to school and collected and once, when the younger two, both girls, were sickly, he had volunteered to collect the boy and walk him home.

"I had finished my night shift at the hospital and had breakfast on my way home. Her car was outside the school and the two little ones were wrapped up on the back seat. She'd had to bring them – couldn't leave them alone, she told me."

That afternoon, when he took the boy home – walking of course – he had been invited in for tea. His own dog was with him and, at first, he had worried about upsetting the huge hounds, but he need not have worried. "The dogs walked round and round each other a few times, then settled down," Theo told them, smiling. "I was mightily relieved, I can tell you."

He had never hesitated to walk his dog near the cottages, after that, even when the compound gate was open. The dogs were always loose during daytime, except at weekends, and 'woofed' a welcome.

One must have died, shortly before the kidnapping, as he stopped appearing, but the other was a loyal guard dog, hardly ever taking its eyes off the children. If chained to its kennel at the back, it meant that the man of the house was at home. Theo supposed that with him there, the dog was off duty!

By the time they left, Theo was exhausted.

He couldn't remember when he'd talked so much and had enjoyed having company.

He knew he could count on them to carry out their promise to visit him again soon, and Sarah, a lovely woman about his own age, said he might be able to help her – she knew she could count on his discretion...

Yes, they were her very words.

17. Add One Angry Man

As soon as they arrived home, Polly started preparing dinner and then sat to add to her notes while the potatoes boiled.

Although the probable identity of the 'kitchen lady' had been established they were a long way away from answers that might help both the living and the dead. She couldn't get it out of her head – the image of the distressed woman, searching for her lost children. How can she ever be persuaded that Dave's grandchildren are not her own little ones? They must be fully grown now, just as Elly's brother Jamie is... Pete and Peggy Fletcher had every reason to be frightened for their young family.

Knowing now what they were up against, perhaps Sarah would offer to babysit soon. It suddenly struck Polly that without delay she should take up Kevin the car-dealer's offer of an introduction to his father.

According to his card his surname was Jones, and, on the back, he had scribbled 'Glyn', followed by a telephone number. Without wasting a moment for second thoughts Polly dialled. Only as she waited for it to be answered did she wonder whether Sarah might have liked to call him herself. Too late – a deep, rich voice answered, "Jones speaking."

He had obviously been briefed by Kevin and did not hesitate to speak of his friend. "My old mate, Denny Davies, is pleased as punch to hear that somebody is willing to look into the case again – he still can't get the sight of the poor woman out of his head. It will do him good to talk about it."

Polly was amazed and delighted to hear that the man was willing, even eager, to go over his awful experience and she made a note of his name and contact details. This time, she would definitely consult Sarah, who would undoubtedly want to speak to him personally.

The couple who had worked for the owner of the farm were Mr and Mrs Ball. Polly had already identified their address and 'phone number. Having rung them, although they were sure they would not be able to help with any information about Mr Simpson, they were intrigued enough to invite Polly and her friend for tea...

"Bill and I would be pleased to talk to you – how about four-o-clock tomorrow," the woman said breathlessly, in a high-pitched, squeaky voice. Polly said she would ask her friend, Sarah, and ring straight back if they needed to change the date or time.

On the spur of the moment, Polly asked if they had heard anything from, or about Mr Simpson since he moved away.

Mrs Ball hesitated, then said quickly that he hadn't contacted them, "But there are always people who hear things, aren't there?" she added, "and then repeat things, but I never listen to gossip." Polly knew better than to comment and just said that she looked forward their meeting.

Over dinner, Polly brought Sarah up to date with her research and Sarah had to admit that young Elly's presence had been so distracting since they came home, that she hadn't been able to focus on anything else.

The child was beginning to understand that she was not in the right place, but she would not even talk about her grandparents who, Sarah guessed, might also be in spirit now. Until she had found Elly's brother, Sarah couldn't hope to connect with any of her loved ones in the spirit world, unless Elly herself opened a channel for her.

Sarah appreciated that the problem of the ghostly dog was more pressing and made Polly laugh when she described how she had made sure that Elly would leave her in peace for a while. "I asked her to go to Clarrie and help her to draw pictures of everything she could remember about her home, her parents, and the place where the strange lady had taken Jamie."

Polly wondered how Clarrie had reacted, but Sarah assured her that they had hatched the plot together. "Clarrie understands the importance of pinpointing a particular area and is quite excited by the idea."

Polly had also established that their 'Kitchen Lady', assuming Theo was right, was Mary Perry. When the three children disappeared, they were about the same ages as the Fletcher children. The father, Elvis, had re-married and was still living within twenty miles of the old cottage.

"I can't imagine that we will ever want, or need, to talk to him," Polly sighed, "Poor, poor man. What a terrible experience to go through – and he would not wish to be reminded of it, I'm sure."

Just beyond her grasp, as Polly reiterated much of what they already knew, Sarah sensed that someone was desperately trying to speak with her – she felt it to be an immediate reaction to their conversation. It was a distraught man who was so angry he was choking on his words.

Polly went silent, seeing Sarah's head turn away with a worried frown creasing her usually smooth face but Sarah assured her that they could not handle any more problems for the moment.

Not until Sarah had described what she had experienced would Polly relax, but Sarah could only say that the man had been standing in front of something that looked like a factory. She hadn't heard much of what he was shouting – only the words *accident* and *rice* were clear …less clearly, she heard *rabies*.

Sighing heavily Polly started to clear the table and protested when despite her claims that she was able to manage, Sarah insisted on helping. When they ended up having coffee in the kitchen Polly had to admit that it had 'saved her legs'!

In a more relaxed mood, Polly recalled several items of gossip she had picked up from Harry and Kevin. "I think I know why the new owner of the farm decided to sell up and move away. I didn't add it to my notes because it doesn't seem relevant now."

Sarah nodded when Polly asked if she recalled the other boys who had disappeared…

"Well, somebody who cleans at the police station found a scan of an email behind the copier …it was informing them that Arthur Simpson, a suspected paedophile, had moved into the area. She told a friend in confidence!"

Sarah's reaction, as Polly expected, was shock that the information should have been leaked and very real sympathy for the man, not proven guilty and obviously trying to make a new life for himself.

Everything they had heard about Arthur Simpson indicated that he was succeeding in putting his past behind him, but after very few years of happiness he had been deprived of his chance by local gossip-mongers. When she rang Alec Holme to check for an update on Elly and her brother she would mention Arthur to him.

Later, Polly recounted her visit to Kevin, still feeling sorry for Arthur, she had commented on his generosity in continuing the arrangement the previous owner had made, allowing the annual lease on the three cottages to remain intact.

Of course, the other two families soon left but Mary's family was not being pressed to move on – he treated them kindly.

Kevin had agreed and started talking about having known Mary and her husband for years, saying how devoted they were and how he always carried snapshots of the children on him to show to anyone who would listen!

Polly sighed.

"Then he went on about their problems when the farmer decided to sell. Even though he let them stay in the cottage, it wasn't easy working away." After all this chat, about Mary being unhappy, being alone all day, Polly had realised her mind was miles away... "He was suddenly talking about having known Elvis Perry at school. They hadn't had much in common then, apparently – Perry was a magnet for the girls but didn't like having competition around! He said their paths had not crossed again until they were adults."

Polly confessed to Sarah that the conversation had become boring, and she lost track. "He started telling me how amazed he was when Perry married her, and I didn't find out why because we were interrupted by a customer," Polly sighed. "Why was he amazed? She seemed quite attractive in the photo we saw."

"Well, it must have been a happy marriage, as they had three lovely children," Sarah commented, and immediately felt that she was missing something.

They must make a point of discovering more about the marriage; it might bring her closer to the Kitchen Lady. Deciding it was a good idea, she suggested that Polly should volunteer their babysitting service the next time Pete and Peggy needed a night out.

It was not too late to ring Gavin and, without hesitation, he offered them his babysitting slot on Saturday night. He and Dave had intended to give up a darts match rather than allow his daughters to go there again.

Their diary was fast getting out of hand, Polly reflected, as she entered yet another appointment. In addition to all the people she wished to speak to herself, she must give Sarah the contact number for Denny Davies. Perhaps they could visit him after they had had

tea tomorrow with Mrs Ball. She made a note to herself…
She would ring the local paper to discover if the reporter
who interviewed Denny was still working there.

It was a long shot, but she would never know if she
didn't ask!

18. Mutual Friends

Polly was satisfied that things were working out well.

The reporter *('just call me Scoop')* who had interviewed Denny Davies was seventy and retired – still living locally and eager to talk about the case... He said he was still in touch with Denny so wondered if they should visit him together. Sarah couldn't see why not, but when Polly checked, Denny said he usually went to bed early and would rather that they did not call on him after seeing the Balls on Friday, so Sarah invited them both for lunch on Sunday, instead.

Thursdays were always quiet at home on Sarah's Bridge morning as she usually stayed out for lunch with her Bridge partner, when there was nothing urgent to do. Today, Sarah was unlikely to return before 5pm, as lunch was often followed by a little window shopping.

Remembering the woman in the library who she had met by accident, and then neglected to contact again, Polly decided to ring her. Perhaps they could meet there again this afternoon. Polly enjoyed browsing in the library and had books to return anyway, so she searched her notes for the telephone number and dialled the stranger to introduce herself to the elderly Mercy Swann.

She reasoned that there must be other locals who

remembered the old farm and its long-gone owner. If she could pick up more 'gossip', before she heard what Mrs Ball had to say, it wouldn't hurt and might help.

Amazingly, it transpired that Mrs Swann knew of her existence already and would be delighted to meet her. She hoped Polly would bring Sarah with her... "I've heard all about Sarah. We have a mutual friend ...I believe you know Maud too." Polly smiled – pleased to hear of the connection but doubting that Maud would have communicated anything significant about Sarah to any other of her friends. Not only was she the soul of discretion, but Maud was constantly on guard against eavesdroppers and, in public, hardly ever raised her voice above a whisper.

"I'm sure Sarah would be very happy to meet you sometime, Mrs Swann, but I was hoping we could meet at the library this afternoon, unless you're busy."

"Let's be Mercy and Polly," was the firm response, "and I will be there at three-thirty, if that suits you." It had sounded almost like a command, Polly thought, but she didn't mind ...perhaps Mercy fancied herself to be senior in age. The idea pleased Polly and made her feel quite sprightly as she carried the library books out to her car.

After shopping and having a lunchtime snack, there was still time to explore the library's newspaper archives to see any editions that had covered the disappearance of the three children. She found very few references to the other children who had interested them – mostly conjecture – but there was an article about the devastated husband whose stricken wife had survived a savage beating. When she had first recovered consciousness, after two days in intensive care, he had been with her, but she wouldn't stop screaming, not recognising him, and had to be sedated again.

It happened every time she opened her eyes and the doctors gave him no hope that her brain injuries could be repaired – that she would ever recover her memory and be normal – so after a week or so, during which time he hardly left her bedside, Elvis Perry left the village and took lodgings nearer to his place of work. At first, he returned frequently to check on his wife and the cottage but, having no hope of Mary's recovery, he gave up. The trail of the attacker had grown cold and without any hope of an interview with the demented wife, the papers had gradually lost interest in him.

With photo-copies of these stories tucked into her shopping bag, Polly met Mercy and they went up in the lift to enjoy tea and an excellent view from the café on the third floor.

Within minutes, Mercy was into at least her third saga about Maud and her younger sister, Norma …who had, "*so tragically died.*"

It was evident that she had been closer to Norma, as they had been in the same school year; speaking of her brought Mercy near to tears. Polly recalled quite clearly that the tragic accident, about seven or eight years ago, was of Norma's own making and Sarah had succeeded in concealing the truth from Maud.

"Norma told me about Sarah being psychic and, although Maud would never believe it, Norma had second sight too – it surprises me that Sarah didn't show more interest in her. Norma was extremely hurt." Mercy mopped her eyes and shook her head. "Perhaps I should avoid meeting Sarah, after all, she might not like to answer some of the questions I would need to ask!"

"Not at all," Polly was quick to say, "Sarah would prefer talking to you, rather than have you fretting about the past, in any way."

Attempting to turn the conversation away from the two sisters, Polly asked if she'd lived in the area all her life and, if so, had she known the family that used to farm the land before it was sold to Arthur Simpson...

To cut Mercy's tale short, when Polly repeated it to Sarah later, Mercy hadn't been to the farm at all, until 'Dear Arthur' started planning how he would convert the primitive, old house into one suitable for guests. He didn't go into the village often, but they had conversed when she left one of her shopping bags in the coffee shop and, as she walked away, he called her attention to it. In gratitude, she insisted that he came for dinner that night and met her husband. He had not yet made many friends in the area and she was pleased to say that the two men found they had interests in common.

Mercy deplored the awful gossip about Arthur – she couldn't believe any of it, he had a heart of gold and would never hurt a child. Most of what went on at the cottages was visible from his property, as the only road access to them ran near his study window and he worried a lot at first about the three children being alone with the dogs until he saw how protective they were. They behaved most threateningly towards Perry, which was why they were only free of their chains when he was not at home.

Mercy glanced around, as if to ensure that no one was near enough to hear and said that if there had been two dogs on guard there would have been no abduction. She described how, a few weeks before that tragic attack on poor Mary, Arthur had seen Perry striking the boy and the larger of the dogs went berserk – howling with anger and pulling on the chain that held him, unable to break it.

Perry had laughed at the dog as he pushed the boy into the house. The fierce barking and howling continued well into the night until there was yelp and sudden silence. Arthur suspected that the dog, having seen Perry strike the boy, had tried to attack Perry at the first opportunity. He was convinced the poor animal had been 'put down' as it was never seen again.

The obviously voluble Arthur had told her that Perry never took his share of babysitting the children – always out drinking. Mercy stressed again how upset Arthur was when children or animals were mistreated. "Poor Mary! Of course, Perry only married her for the money..." Only when repeating the conversation to Sarah, did Polly regret not following up on that comment but, at the time, Mercy had launched into a detailed description of Arthur's plans for his new home.

They eventually parted with Mercy promising to ring Polly ...they must both come to dinner soon! Sarah smiled wryly, from the sound it, discussing 'Poor Norma' would no doubt be high on the agenda.

19. A Gruesome Find

Neighbours in the road where Minnie Travis and Dora Mace lived next door to each other were all agog to see a police car at Dora's gate. Those who were not standing open-mouthed or gossiping over walls, were twitching their curtains to discover what was happening.

Minnie was inside trying to comfort Dora, who was clearly bewildered by what was going on. A policewoman sat with them quietly in the front room while her male colleagues filled every other corner of her home. They tramped endlessly up and down the stairs and sealed off the attic until a forensic team arrived to investigate whatever it was that the plumber had discovered up there.

Dora's mind, closed for so long even to the existence of the loft, darted disjointedly through the years since she had been blessed with her darling Joe. Her husband had left her to cope alone with her baby who seemed always to be ill – and she had coped well; he had recovered, hadn't he? ...and grown into a fine young man. Joe had loved being near the sea... She had promised to take him, she remembered... *Was that the day he wouldn't wake up?* No, it couldn't have been, she had dressed him in new blue shorts...

She vaguely remembered having been shocked all

those years ago when the doorbell rang... *The doctor: he wouldn't understand; he would take Joe away – the poor baby would be so frightened – she had to hide him!* In a daze, all that Dora was sure of now was that Joe had been paddling in the sea and she pulled him out and ...*and the sea had cured him ...and he could walk!* It was wonderful; he grew stronger every day.

The plumber telephoned Minnie immediately after he called the police. Under the overflowing water tank, wrapped in a soggy, wet blanket, which was falling apart with age were the remains of a small body. The man was still in shock, white-faced and shaking, when Minnie came to help him with Dora, who was frozen to the spot, staring at him open-mouthed. She must have heard his call to the police, but he said she hadn't moved, or spoken, since he hung up.

After leading Dora into her sitting room and making sure she was comfortable, she took the plumber to the kitchen and asked him to boil the kettle to make tea for them all. He needed to be given any kind of task to occupy his mind, she thought, then grabbing a warm blanket from the airing cupboard she hastened back to tuck it round her friend.

Dora was still staring into the distance, eyes glazed, so Minnie tried to bring her back to her present situation. Horrific as it was, the police interrogation would be more ruthless than she thought Dora deserved. Her own memories of the sickly little boy were of him in his wheelchair, watching Dora hanging out laundry to dry. When she finished she would always lift Joe onto the grass trying to walk him round, pointing out flowers, birds or insects – anything to make him smile.

He did smile and even laughed sometimes, but he was obviously weak, and Minnie's heart went out to him and his poor mother. One day, when Joe was not with Dora, Minnie enquired about the child and was told that the doctor had advised her to let him rest – not to overtire him for a few days, but he was quite happy.

During the following weeks all Minnie's offers to sit with Joe, so that Dora could rest or go shopping, were refused. Partly to clarify her own memory of those far off days, Minnie took Dora's hand and said, "Joe was so weak and ill when you came here. I think you said the doctor might want to move him to hospital." Dora stared steadily as though not understanding, then, slowly, she brightened.

"Yes – I was so frightened that they would take him away and not bring him back ...but they didn't ...so he was able to sleep and get better..." Dora's eyes closed, and she appeared to drift to sleep. Slowly she began to whisper, as if talking to herself... "I'd promised to take him to the seaside – he always loved it when I walked him through the water, but he wouldn't wake up for me to take him." Minnie was shocked – it was easy now to guess what happened, but how? She could only murmur sympathetically and wait.

"I pushed the chair down to the edge of the water. I'd been right about the sea being the best thing for him." Dora, smiling, eyes still closed, was remembering being on the sandy beach and stopping to lift Joe from his chair... "I was shocked when it was empty," she said, "but straight away I saw him in the water with a girl

…she must have snatched him when my back was turned but there he was, trying to crawl back to me, the waves rolling around him, so I ran to take his hand. The girl stretched out, trying to pull him back, but I was too quick."

When she lapsed into silence Minnie risked speaking. "So, you brought him home," she said quietly. Dora said nothing for several minutes, but it was obvious that her thoughts were in turmoil. Minnie and policewoman exchanged shrugs and waited until Dora relaxed and smiled.

"Joe wouldn't stay in his chair – it was wonderful to see him walking, and we both laughed and cried, all the way home. We had tea and played until bath-time and I left him sitting in the bath, watching the water draining away, while I went to his room to fetch his pyjamas and his favourite bla… blan…"

Up to that moment Dora had looked ecstatic but, in seconds, things changed. Clutching her head in her hands – she stood abruptly, staring up at the ceiling and gave a piercing scream.

A week later, Alec Holme was in his study looking through emails on his home-computer before leaving for the office, when his wife, Jessica, rushed in, waving her hometown newspaper *The Ormskirk Advertiser*, which had just arrived by post. "Look, it's only a snippet, but it could be what you have been looking for – a child's body in an attic!"

Startled more by her noisy entrance rather than her words, Alec read the report with interest. The little that was in it was all relevant... The body had been hidden for over twenty years and was that of a boy about three or four years old. Jessica offered him the paper to take with him, but he would be able to obtain much more information officially.

He was pleased that her sharp eyes had spotted it and Jessica, happy to have helped, decided to text family and friends back home to pick up on the gossip. Commenting on his way out, Alec said there was no harm in Jessica alerting Sarah about the news item. "With her contacts, she might well be able to get the details more quickly than I can!"

Sarah was pleased to hear from Jessica and intrigued to learn about the discovery of a child's body in Formby. It was almost lunchtime and it was obvious that Jessica had spent the morning chasing up every scrap of information that was on the 'grapevine'. "Well, whether it is the little boy whose disappearance we know about or not, Jess, he was somebody's child and I will do my best to follow up on everything you've discovered."

After listening again, she answered, "Yes, it's an excellent idea to email everything to me – I have been trying to take notes, but you have said so much between the lines that my memory will be sorely taxed, and I can't risk missing something vital."

Later, after the email arrived she would tell Polly, but first she decided to deal with all the mail that was already stacking up, both on her computer and on the doormat!

20. Letters from Spain

Sarah's mind was whirling, trying to make sense of the conflicting information that Polly had noted... Elvis Perry was said to be happy and caring by some people, yet others, particularly Mercy Swann, implied otherwise. Not only was he indifferent to the children, but she said he'd married for money!

Another vision kept flashing through her mind every time she thought of the missing children; she was inside a car in a raging storm and the windscreen wipers were not coping. It would have been frightening anyway but, although she had never driven a car, she was at the wheel, steering blindly. Shuddering, she pulled her thoughts back to the present and clicked on her inbox...

Immediately, she saw that two messages had attachments – one from Clarrie and the promised one from Jessica Holme, which she opened first. Whatever information it held could be forwarded to Clarrie. The various comments by neighbours were in a numbered list – very efficient, Sarah smiled; Jessica was clearly used to helping Alec with his notes. All the comments were similar and agreed that the little boy was thin, pale and wobbly when they moved in and then nobody saw him for a few weeks... When they did, he was healthy and happily running about.

An elderly resident, now in her eighties was particularly upset. Her own mother, until the day she died, maintained that she saw Dora Mace walking to the bus stop with an empty pushchair. She was so concerned that she hurried to Dora's neighbour, but she was out. Standing in the deserted street, unable to decide whether to ring the police, in case the child was alone inside, she was nearly in tears. A friend, out walking her dog, tried to comfort her, unable to believe that the lovely Dora, who she knew well, would leave Joe on his own. She had persuaded the old lady to go home and tell her daughter, who was sure to know what to do.

The daughter in question was now old herself and mortified, remembering how they had all ridiculed the idea that anyone would push an empty pram to the beach. They had kept watch for the bus and, eventually, saw Dora return with the boy. It was obvious that she had not left him alone and because, amazingly, he was walking, they decided he must have run on ahead when going for the bus. Everyone on the street was delighted at the boy's return to health.

The attachments were photographs of the house, taken by a reporter, with the address pencilled at the bottom of each; one pictured the front, from the open gate, and one had been cheekily snapped through a half-open window. There was not much to see inside but a net curtain was blowing open to reveal the mantelpiece and, beyond it, a piano.

After replying, sending her thanks quickly, Sarah opened the email from her daughter and read:

'Automatic drawings. Goodness only knows how much help I had'... There were five pictures attached and as she clicked through them, opening every one, her excitement grew.

Polly came into their office urging Sarah to hurry, as Mrs Ball was expecting them in twenty minutes but, as soon as she understood what Sarah was doing, she ceased to nag and pulled up a chair. The sketches were like nothing Clarrie had ever drawn before – broken, hesitant lines and false starts were visible, but Clarrie had obviously gone over those she thought likely to be more relevant on the last two pictures. It was clear that all were attempts to portray the same things ...a piano and a doorway.

Opening Jessica's email again, Sarah showed Polly the two photographs she had sent. There was no doubt that the door in the sketch was the front door of the house; the pattern on the wall matched the brickwork and the letterbox was in the same position. The clincher was the pot-plant near the step.

The second drawing appeared to be a face on a shelf, standing next to an animal. When they enlarged the area beyond the curtain, in the second of Jessica's photos, they saw a framed photograph of a boy and a porcelain cat. They were standing together on top of a piano.

"Why do people do that?" Polly asked, not really seeking an answer. "No real pianist lives in that house! Ornaments would shake"

Sarah was more concerned that Elly's brother must have grown up in it, unaware that he didn't really belong there. She was sure this was a fact and telephoned Alec immediately. The young man, apparently called Joe, must be informed as soon as possible that not only had he been abducted but that steps were already being taken to find his natural parents. Sarah added that she would welcome the opportunity to speak privately with him, feeling sure that she would be able to offer him some comfort. Alec agreed and promised to relay her invitation to the boy, with his personal recommendation that he would not regret meeting Sarah.

Before ringing off, Sarah asked if Arthur Simpson was still listed as a possible paedophile and, because he was not (and never had been), Alec was able to pass the information on without compromising his position. It was a relief and important to know this before they met Mr and Mrs Ball.

21. Tea for Four

They were only a polite five minutes late; perfect timing. Sarah firmly believed that for social invitations it was bad manners to be early and wrong to arrive on time. It is unlikely that anyone hosting a private affair would not be ready for the time stated, but they usually relished a few minutes breathing space to take stock of the scene that would greet their guests.

Mrs Ball invited them in with a beaming smile and introduced her husband Bill to them, adding that she was Barbie, which made their email address easy to remember… '*bbball*'. Laughing, they were soon all on first-name terms. Sarah was glad she had confirmed with Alec Holme that Arthur Simpson really had been cleared of wrongdoing and shared Barbie's disgust at the rumour-mongers gossip, which drove him away.

Apart from liking him, Barbie was personally disappointed because she and Bill had enjoyed working in such a comfortable well-paid job. More like a friend than an employer, Arthur sometimes accompanied Bill when he walked the fields for exercise – picking mushrooms being a fine excuse to get out in the fresh air.

"Did you ever walk as far as the cottages?" Sarah asked. "I believe the dogs were quite fierce."

"They were more protective than fierce," Bill said, "...especially if the children were outside playing. Of course, they were always chained up when their father was home," – he laughed, "the dogs I mean! I can understand why, especially after only one dog was left. He hated Elvis – snarled at him, even lunging at the end of his chain to attack him. Elvis just laughed and drove off to work in his car.

His wife set the animals free then and one day, seeing me hunting for mushrooms on the other side of the fence, she said that the dogs would stay unchained until her husband was due home, but I need not worry, even if the gate was open they wouldn't leave their compound. She said the problem was that Elvis was nervous and animals always know, don't they?" Polly smiled ...*it must be true – she'd heard that before!*

Polly seized the opportunity to introduce the unfortunate abduction of the three children and the other boys whose disappearance had sparked the rumours about Arthur. Bill and Barbie could only mourn the unfairness of it all. "The first thing he did, when he bought the place, was to have mains water supplied to the cottages. Since their well had dried up, they'd had to collect water from the fresh springs. Mind you we sometimes fill a churn there ourselves, it tastes so pure."

"He was a kind man," Bill interrupted to stem her flow, "and only after we walked near the cottage, and saw how gentle the dogs were with the children, did he stop worrying about them. When we drew closer, both dogs went into a crouch and snarled their heads off! We kept well away after that and less than a month later only one dog was there – I don't know what happened to the other eventually."

Barbie interrupted to say that it had happened around about the time the boy was drowned …less than a month before the abduction. Both dogs had barked incessantly all through one night until the barks changed to growls and howls. "It sounded as if they had started fighting each other – then, at sun up, nothing. Arthur and I saw Elvis driving to work a few hours later. He slowed down to apologise if we'd been disturbed and said it wouldn't happen again."

They knew little else about the terrace of cottages except that they were enclosed together, on about two acres of land and Arthur had planned to replace them with one large house eventually. There was plenty to be done before that happened, so he was quite happy for the young family to stay there in exchange for keeping the ground tidy and doing their own repairs.

Before Arthur left, they heard that the runaway boy had been found near his old home and was being fostered by a neighbouring couple. Happily, able to attend his old school, he was extremely unlikely to run away again. The body of the boy believed to have drowned was never found. A cap identified as his had blown along the main road from the river and was picked up near the lane leading to the farm. It was this fact that had leaked out and fed the gossipmongers.

Sarah was suddenly distracted when the earlier vision flashed to her mind again …windscreen wipers fighting a losing battle against the storm… There had to be a connection, but to what? The boy, Arthur or Perry?

The police were satisfied that the boy's disappearance was nothing to do with Arthur but had no reason to issue a statement of denial because they had never officially named Arthur Simpson as a suspect. It was therefore impossible for him to feel comfortable about settling in the area.

"It was all so long ago," sighed Barbie, "and at the time we were already concerned about Arthur's feelings and didn't want to dwell on the horror of what had happened so close by." Bill leaned across and patted her hands, which were clenched on her lap.

He assured them that the fine weather at the time of the abduction meant that all windows and doors were open until they went to bed, so anyone approaching the cottages would have had to pass within view, whether by car or on foot. "We neither saw nor heard anything suspicious; in fact, it had been very quiet all day. Unlike the weekend when the dogs kept us awake all night."

"Oh, yes," Barbie interrupted. "It was my birthday on the third of March and we had dinner out, as a treat. We were so tired, but the dogs kept us awake." For which he apologised on his way to work, Bill reminded her... "Well, so he should. But things did change. Soon after he came home from work, in the late afternoon, I saw him in the garden with the kids. They were rigging up some kind of tent – really happy."

Arthur too was pleased to see that Perry was taking more interest in the children and they appeared to be building a sort of shelter. They were leaning planks against the fence and using blankets or something similar. Whatever it was, they seemed to enjoy sitting in it. When they weren't, they could have been anywhere, as the rear of all three properties was then hidden.

The three cottages were angled so that all the fronts could be seen from the old farmhouse but only the side garden and the rear of the nearest. As the other two were empty, the children and dogs had plenty of play-space to enjoy and the front of the compound was a huge vegetable patch and parking space for several vehicles.

"Was that the week before the abduction? Sarah asked. Barbie couldn't be sure whether it was one or two, or even the same weekend that the gruesome crime was committed. As she said, they had tried to put the whole ghastly affair out of their minds.

Bill did recall, in particular, one question that the police had asked. "They wanted to know whether we had noticed what time the cottage lights came on."

"Yes, that's right," Barbie agreed, "and funnily enough, we hadn't."

Sarah and Polly exchanged glances ...both realising that the lights would only become evident when darkness came – they could have been on all day!

Later at home they wondered, if he had left the lights on, where was his wife? Would she have taken the children out and returned without them? ...Unlikely and, anyway, he spoke to her when he left didn't he?

Sarah, not wanting to outstay their welcome, had attempted to leave several times, but their hosts were reluctant to end the discussion. They may have thought they would hear something new, although it was more likely that, after bottling up their feelings for so long, it was a relief to talk it through. They interrupted each other frequently, but Polly managed to add to her notes.

Soon after *The Grocer's Arms* shut, on that long-ago Saturday night, the car returned to drop Elvis back home and the commotion began. There were police and ambulance sirens, every inch teeming with officials, followed by reporters and curious villagers. There had been no rest for anyone, either that night or the following day. The police were ever-present asking questions and searching the lane for clues. It seemed impossible that three children could have been removed from their beds without causing them to scream or cry...

"And why didn't the dog bark?" Barbie wanted to know. "It's a puzzle to me why the dog didn't attack the intruders before they even reached the front door."

"The dog was chained apparently," Polly suddenly remembered someone commenting on it.

"Yes, of course," Bill said, "Perry was so scared of it that his wife only allowed it to roam free when his car drove off and he always hooted his horn as he arrived home, to make sure it was chained again!"

Sarah and Polly exchanged meaningful glances – both wondering why no explanation had yet been put forward for its being chained during the attack. "Could someone who knew their system have tooted?" Polly asked. "She'd have chained it again, so the kidnapper would have had nothing to worry about." Bill didn't think so; a vehicle would have had to pass twice. There was no way they would have missed it, especially if the horn had sounded.

There was little else forthcoming about the horrific

event and nothing about the young family's background, as the Balls were relatively new to the neighbourhood at the time. Of course, everyone was eager to talk with them during the distressful investigation and by the time their employer moved away, and the place sold, they had enough friends in the area to make staying there feasible.

Later, back home, Sarah was keen to go over all Polly's notes – adding a few of her own.

While Polly brought their diary up to date, Sarah was wrapped in thought. She was concerned that the dog was chained when Perry returned with his mate on Saturday night. His wife had been almost beaten to death hours earlier, so if she had not had time to set the dog free after he left, the attack on her must have been immediately on his departure. It didn't make sense. That the children had been moved without their having made a sound could only mean that they were drugged. Ruling out their parents, who else could have done it?

It occurred to Sarah that Theo might know more about Perry's background and they would have an opportunity to ask him very soon, as he was eager to baby-sit with them tomorrow. Every mention of Perry immediately brought to her mind the vision she'd had of the angry man.

Perhaps if she relaxed for a few minutes he might appear to her again. In his distress, his words were unclear and although it went against her instinct to invite contact from the 'other side', she was always ready to help if she could.

The words she'd heard revolved in her mind as she closed her eyes and relaxed – *accident ...rice ...rabies.*

Polly thought she was asleep and hesitated about staying with her, but Sarah opened her eyes and explained. There had been no opportunity to speak of her vision before and it was significant enough to note, as part of the mystery.

Filling her files with more facts always made Polly happy and she scribbled rapidly while Sarah talked.

It was obviously going to be another late night, but they were both reluctant to part before all their new information was explored.

22. Babysitting

Pete Fletcher and his wife Peggy had not raised any objections to Theo Penn accompanying the baby-sitters. On the contrary, they thought it an excellent idea to have a man on hand. Sarah refrained from pointing out that the ghostly hound only attacked men... Theo knew and was not perturbed, in fact he was hoping to see the animal for himself.

They were not going out until after the children were tucked up in their beds, so Peggy took Polly up to see them. Standing in the connecting doorway – in the children's hearing – she warned that all pleas for food, drink or for more stories to be read to them must be ignored. They just giggled and pretended to be upset.

Sarah and Theo waited quietly, both hoping that the 'kitchen lady' would make her presence known. "I suppose there is no doubt in your mind that she is Mary Bryce," said Theo.

"None at all," Sarah replied. "This house stands exactly where the cottages were. Their back garden opened onto the open field, as this one does, and beyond, to our left is the older property where Arthur Simpson once lived. You did say that Mary kept returning to look for her children. It seems likely that when she eventually found three children here, similar in ages to those she lost, she convinced herself that she was at home. She probably doesn't see the place as it is now... She sees it as it lingers in her memory and she has no concept of the time lapse. It will be a tremendous shock to be suddenly shocked into reality again, and we have to help her to come to terms with what happened."

Sarah suddenly registered that Theo had said Mary Bryce, not Perry. The name struck a chord in her own memory, but she was sure she had not come across it before. Before she could query the name, Theo realised his mistake and said, "Sorry – of course you must think of her as Mary Perry, but I knew the family when the children were all babies, before their father died."

That was it; the angry man in her vision was not shouting *rice rabies* he was saying 'Bryce' and 'babies' and something about an accident. When she explained, Theo was excited and eager to explain that Mary's first husband, Geoff Bryce, lost his labouring job when the farm ceased to function; he went to work in a factory. They still had the cottage, of course, and he was earning more at the factory than he had before, so all went well until his accident. Some machinery had malfunctioned, and Geoff was crushed.

Polly returned with Peggy, who waved to them as she hurried out to join her husband, impatiently waiting in the car. Seeing Sarah's face, Polly knew that something had brought a spark of excitement to her eyes but held back from making any comment. Instead she passed on Peggy's message, that there was a light supper in the fridge and they must help themselves to whatever they wished to drink.

Sarah smiled as Theo sprang to his feet and offered to be barman; for him, it was a rare, social evening with new friends.

Sarah brought Polly up-to-date with her discovery and, when he returned with their drinks, they could hardly wait for him to settle down. Polly was mortified – Kevin the car must have been speaking of Geoff's death when her thoughts had drifted, and she had not been paying attention and misunderstood when Kevin had expressed surprise that Elvis married her...

They now had a string of questions... *Had Geoff and Elvis been friends? Had Mary known Elvis, before her husband died?* Theo didn't know how close Elvis was to the family – but it didn't surprise him that Mary remarried within six months. Left to cope alone with three children must have been frightening and very hard. There was not much he could add, and he was more eager to discuss the current haunting that they were investigating.

Sarah suggested that they should do nothing out of the ordinary but cast their minds occasionally to Mary and her children, making it easy for her to appear to them, if she wished. As she spoke, Sarah was aware that another little lost soul was present. Elly was trying to tell her something, growing impatient. "Why won't the lady upstairs talk to *me*? I can see her and hear her, and they can't but she still keeps talking to *them*!"

"Could you take me to her, Elly?" Polly and Theo listened open-mouthed to Sarah, but neither saw the child. They watched as Sarah rose and walked from the room, to the bottom of the stairs. "Could you please try, now, to bring the lady to me?" After a long pause Sarah explained. "We would be able to talk here, without disturbing the children, wouldn't we?" After a few minutes Sarah relaxed and turned to face them. She didn't know if her plan would work – it all depended on whether the 'kitchen lady' really could see and hear Elly. She had never attempted to introduce one spirit to another before!

After several minutes elapsed without anything happening, Sarah felt driven to say, "Let's go and sit down again and see what develops. Even if anything does, it might not be soon – there's no such thing as time in the spirit world, so we may as well wait in comfort!"

The television news broadcast was drawing to an end as they finished the supper Peggy had left for them. Polly's mind was on 'Kevin the Car' and his comment about being surprised when Elvis Perry married Mary. She understood now. Mary had been a widow with three small children; so why *had* he married her?

She made a mental note to contact Mercy Swann. She had said how upset Arthur was by the way Elvis neglected his children – never even appearing to spend time with them. Mercy might have known he was their step-father but considered it common knowledge; her memory, if prodded, might reveal other facts of interest.

Sarah and Theo were considering going upstairs to peep in on the children; he was eager to see if the fearsome ghostly hound would appear to him. It was after ten-o-clock and not having any idea when the parents would return, Sarah agreed.

Polly was happy to remain in the hallway and watch as they started to climb the stairs, Theo leading the way, at his insistence.

They moved slowly and were only a few steps from the top when a low growl echoed from the landing. Polly heard it too – and was thrilled to know that her lately discovered clairaudience had not left her. She swallowed a gasp, anxious not to disturb the atmosphere and both Sarah and Theo paused. Polly could tell that they were both watching the animal. "Oh, my God," whispered Theo, "it's Butcher – the dog that disappeared…"

The growling had grown louder and changed to a vicious snarl as the animal began to crawl nearer to him. Theo stood his ground and held out his hand to within a foot of the demented dog. "Butcher, old boy, you know me. Don't be alarmed; we are friends, aren't we?"

Sarah saw how the dog reacted. Slowly realising that Theo was indeed a friend, he squirmed onto his back and wriggled forward to have his tummy rubbed. As she watched, she had a vision of what must have been the last moments of his life. Covered in blood, his limbs distorted and broken and hardly anything left of his eyes and head. She grasped the banister rail and gasped in distress. Who could have beaten the poor creature so viciously? The answer was obvious – it could only have been Elvis Perry, and it had happened a few weeks before the abduction of the children.

Try as she might, Sarah had not succeeded in making contact with anyone on the 'other side' who would know where they had grown up. They must have had grandparents and their real father …why hadn't they come through to help?

She remembered then that their father *had* appeared to her. Later, in a calmer mood, she would turn over all these problems in her mind and hope he would appear to her again, in a quieter frame of mind than he had the first time. Now, she had to help Theo.

Walking slowly up to where Theo was petting the dog, Sarah risked holding out her own hand and, to her relief he rolled over and sniffed it, before pushing his nose under it and sliding it up to his ears to be patted.

When he stood and turned away, it was to greet Elly, who was obviously thrilled to have contacts in a world where she had been alone. Slowly materialising behind her was Mary. She took Elly's hand, pulled her away protectively and the dog followed...

Theo and Sarah were then alone on the landing, unwilling to leave, but not quite knowing whether they should stay. For several minutes, they stood undecided and were thrilled when Elly appeared again. Mary, beside her, stared first at Sarah then at Theo until he spoke to her, not able to stand the tension. "I'm Theo Penn, your friend. When we first met, you were Mrs Bryce and I walked your little boy home from school."

Mary frowned, her face creased in puzzlement...

It seemed an age before she relaxed and gave a tentative smile.

Still obviously confused, she glanced back to Sarah, as if waiting to be introduced. Sarah was glad of the opportunity to talk to her – she must be brought out of her dream and had to accept that there was another world awaiting her and it was time to move on. Elly too, still clutching her hand, needed to accept that many years had passed since her life on earth had ended. Sarah hoped they could help each other.

"This is my friend Sarah," said Elly. "She is helping me to find my little brother." Sarah smiled but realised that, in Mary's mind, she had found her children and didn't need such help.

She decided to take a chance and said, "I could help you to find Geoff, your husband. Would you like me to try, Mary?" Elly was ecstatic at the idea and held her breath, waiting for Mary to reply.

Mary looked confused and her spirit form wavered, almost disappearing several times but slowly she steadied and spoke for the first time, in a surprisingly strong voice. "How kind... Yes, Geoff ...he would love to see how his babies are growing. I think he must have gone away, but it isn't like him not to tell me... It's all so confusing – why can't I remember?"

"Don't worry about it now. Elly knows where I am, and I will happily try to help if you come to talk to me."

Still looking dazed, but not really upset, Mary nodded as she turned to go back to the bedroom. Elly waved to Sarah and followed her, leaving only the dog on guard. Theo patted Butcher and then descended to Sarah in the hallway. She asked Polly, "While we watch, would you mind going up to check that the children are alright – undisturbed by our chatter?"

"Butcher is still there," said Theo, "but he can't hurt you and it would be interesting to see if he growls ...it really could be that he distrusts only men!"

Polly agreed readily.

Hearing anything supernatural thrilled her, even if it was unfriendly. She knew how to deal with dogs, alive or dead... As she reached the top stair, Sarah warned her that she could see Butcher, lying with his head between his paws – eyes fixed on her – but he made no sound and made no attempt to follow Polly into the girls' bedroom. They were fast asleep, as was their brother in the adjoining room. When she emerged, he did nothing until she started walking down again, whereupon he rolled on his side and appeared to go to sleep.

Well, the question was answered – female babysitters had nothing to fear. Whether this would persuade Gavin to allow her granddaughters to volunteer again, Polly couldn't predict, but she thought not.

23. The Other Dog

When they returned home, having said goodnight to Theo, at his door, Polly made hot milk chocolate – Sarah's favourite drink, when too late for coffee. There was a lot to discuss and they were both too animated to sleep. It was interesting that Theo had immediately known that the dog was Butcher – Polly had assumed that the two animals were the same breed, perhaps brothers.

From what others had said, Sarah thought the other was less aggressive, but all dogs are individual, and Theo hadn't hesitated in identifying him as Butcher. Even so, the other dog was equally feared by Elvis, so why hadn't he barked to protect the family – and what happened to him after there was nobody left to guard?

It was added to Polly's list of questions for Mercy Swann. At least they were beginning to feel more confident about being on the right track. There was also the possibility that Denny and Scoop, who would be coming for lunch tomorrow, would know all the answers. Theo was certain that the accident to Geoff Bryce had been industrial – machinery malfunction or some-such. "If it wasn't his own fault, perhaps the firm had to pay compensation," Polly suggested, "in which case we need look no further into Elvis Perry's willingness to take on a young family!"

"You may have a point," said Sarah, "but we must not rush to judgement." Let's look at the photos I've had from Jess and the drawings that Clarrie did, with Elly's help." As she had expected, discussing the pictures brought Elly to join them. With a nod to Polly, Sarah said, "Hello, Elly – is Mary with you?" Polly tried to follow the exchange by hearing only one side and it was not difficult...

"Of course not. Yes, I understand, Mary won't leave the children at night... So, you like being with her ...I will try to explain where you both are and where you really should be and then I hope you will help me by explaining it to Mary... When she is ready you can go together ...yes, it is a happy place where I think you will find people who know you... No, no, I wouldn't dream of sending you away until you have found Jamie. The picture you drew of the house where he lived with the lady is very good – I saw a real photograph of it."

After half an hour of this one-sided conversation, Sarah sank back into her armchair and raised her feet, with a deep sigh. Polly waited a moment before saying, "It seems that you have made her understand that he lived to grow up and she didn't."

"I think she does, and when I told her that the little boy found in the attic had looked so much like Jamie that his own mother made a terrible mistake, her first thought was for the child who had been forgotten. She wondered if he was like herself, wandering alone somewhere. She hoped he had found someone like me."

Sarah could not help herself ...her eyes filled with tears and she groped for a handkerchief. Thrusting a box of tissues at her and taking one herself, Polly announced that they'd had enough for one day, Sarah needed to get a good night's sleep – what was left of it anyway!

After mopping her eyes, Polly took the tray back to the kitchen to wash up and put the kettle on for hot water bottles… It was the least she could do and looking after Sarah came first.

They both had reason to be happy with the way things were going and she determined to convince Sarah of that, as she went upstairs to put hot bottles in both their beds – it would be a nice surprise for her and hopefully work magic, taking her mind off others for a moment and having a comfortable night.

24. Sunday Lunch

When she awoke the following morning to see Elly sitting on her window seat, quietly waiting to speak with her, Sarah was not surprised. She had already decided to enlist Clarrie's help again as Elly trusted her and loved Emma.

Daxy, who was never far from the baby, wagged his tail whenever he sensed her ghostly presence, so Elly was eager to be with them again. She understood that Clarrie would help her to remember where she had lived with her parents and then she would be able to see them, and everything would be fine because Sarah would tell them that losing Jamie was not her fault …and they would understand.

Elly couldn't quite grasp that she need not be tied to this physical plane, but when she accepted the fact, Sarah would convince her that there was a great adventure ahead in a place where she could be happy. More to the point, she would be able to peep back at this world and visit Clarrie and Sarah, whenever she wished.

Realising that Sarah was awake Elly informed her, eagerly, that Mary was acting very strangely – always searching for things and muttering about them not being where they should be. "She stares at the children and asks funny things," Elly said, "like '*what happened to your hair'* and *'where did you get those funny clothes'..."*

It made Sarah realise that she must talk with Mary very soon. Hopefully, her memory was returning slowly, which would be good but, if it returned suddenly, the shock could drive her to madness. Without delay she rang Clarrie and reminded her that she had better make sure she had MapQuest on her computer – and the starting point was the house where Jamie had grown up.

Being told not to worry and not to fuss, Sarah sighed and hung up. Turning, to suggest that Elly should go, she discovered that the child had already gone! Was she relieved she wondered, or did she feel superfluous? It was not the time to worry, they were expecting guests within a couple of hours.

Not wanting to distract or bother Polly, Sarah kept out of her way and sorted through her emails. She must stop worrying about Elly and concentrate on Mary. It was an encouraging sign that the woman's mind was beginning to open itself to reality but, when full realisation comes, she will have to understand that her children had disappeared so long ago that, wherever they are, they will have few memories of their mother.

A strange sensation came over her – a feeling that they were beyond reach – they had left the earthly plane! It seemed incredible that not one of the three siblings had survived to adulthood. What further tragedy could have overtaken them? She wondered if there was any way Alec could help – but the police must have tried to find them and failed... Really, what was she thinking ...time was getting on ...the man who witnessed the crime scene was coming to lunch but his first-hand account must wait until they finished eating; Polly was an excellent cook and her efforts would not be appreciated if conversation were not kept in a lighter vein.

The doorbell interrupted her thoughts and she hurried to welcome their guests.

When introductions were over, Polly served drinks and settled down to relax – the meal would be ready in twenty minutes, she promised. The two men were eager to discover the reason for their interest in researching the tragedy. There was no point in prevaricating. If either Denny or Scoop scoffed at the notion of a place being haunted, Sarah would find it easy to create some doubt in their minds.

Luckily, Scoop said he had investigated a haunting once and it had been quite scary. He needed little encouragement to explain. Experts maintained that there was no physical explanation for portraits being turned to face the wall or even falling off it. "Poltergeists," Denny agreed with him, "definitely poltergeists."

Sarah was encouraged: one hurdle less to overcome. "So many people find it hard to accept, but you will be pleased to know that this is not that kind of activity." She paused, for effect, then told them about Mary and the dog. They both immediately volunteered to babysit!

At this point Polly hastened to serve lunch, during which they spoke of Mary's first husband. Both had known and liked him. The dreadful accident that befell him was a shock to the whole community. Everyone had worried that his wife would be unable to cope and did what they could, but her cottage was way off the beaten track. Most of them admitted, shamefacedly, that it had been regarded as a blessing when she remarried.

It was no surprise to Sarah that Geoff Bryce was hovering – this time in a quieter frame of mind. He looked sad. Seeing and hearing his friends must have been heart-warming but difficult when he could not communicate with them.

Aware that he had Sarah's attention he was trying, but failing, to tell her something. She could see him growing angry again and, in her thoughts, told him not to try now – there was too much going on. He must come to her when all was quiet; she would be able to listen and would do her best to help him. He shook his head in frustration, but faded out of her sight, with an understanding nod.

Denny said that, until Elvis Perry started courting Mary, he had never met him, but Perry called on her regularly. Taking her out anywhere in the evening would have been difficult, but he did take the children for outings – the Saturday matinee at the local cinema or the park playground, which obviously made a positive impression on their mother. Mary encouraged Denny to invite him out for a drink locally, so he became a familiar figure to the locals in no time.

"She was undoubtedly attractive," said Polly, "but what could have persuaded him to take on another man's family?"

"Well," admitted Scoop, "I did wonder if the insurance money had anything to do with it!" Sarah and

Polly exchanged glances ...they had speculated themselves about that. Scoop confirmed that it was a substantial amount of money. Mary had been advised about investment and a portion of it was tied to the children. Of course, he had no idea what happened after her death, but it was likely that Perry inherited something automatically. Before Geoff died, they were not wealthy ...not the kind of people who worried about leaving wills!

After they'd eaten, settling again in the comfort of the sitting room, Sarah started to draw the net curtains part-way across the bay window to hide the sun's glare, but hesitated and stared at the lane beyond the garden. On the edge of her vision she was sure she had seen a figure – someone just standing, staring at the house. The shadows thrown by the trees were deep and there was no intruder to be seen now, but she pulled the curtains closer than usual, to thwart prying eyes.

Resuming her armchair, Sarah asked if they could clarify what happened on the night of the abduction. Denny took the lead by describing the evening, from the time he picked up Elvis, just after seven-thirty. "He closed the front door and was halfway down the path when he stopped and looked back. He shouted to me that Mary was calling to him, then went to the door again. I turned the car around and pulled past the gate while they exchanged a few words then he hurried to join me, shaking his head and laughing – muttering, *women, women!*"

"Did you hear what she said? Do you think she sounded upset?" Polly asked and was answered, '*no*' to both questions. Denny said that Elvis was in excellent spirits, so it was unlikely that Mary had been anything other than happy about his having a night out. "What happened at the end of the evening?" Polly continued.

"Well, as soon as we saw the cottage we were alarmed because all the lights were on – not just the porch and living room – but upstairs too, front and back, and the front door was ajar. Elvis shouted to me that something must be wrong, could I wait? But I followed him into the house."

"Where was the dog?" Sarah asked.

"Howling at the back," Denny confirmed, "but Mary was lying in the kitchen in a pool of blood and very still. Elvis rushed to her and tried to pick her up, but I knew she shouldn't be moved and yelled at him to go upstairs to check the children while I rang the police and emergency services. He was screaming their names and then, in no time, he came hurtling down, shouting that they were not there. Someone had taken them away...

He kept moaning '*Mary, Mary*' and tried to clutch her again but I'd detected a faint pulse, so I held him back and told him that help was coming." His eyes moistened at the memory as he added, quietly, "Elvis looked stunned and started moaning. That's about it really. The place was soon full of police and ambulance crew, followed by the Press."

He nodded at Scoop, who had little to add really, but he'd brought with him his collection of photographs, all taken that night, at the scene. He said they were duplicates and could be kept to study later. He, and his editor, had noticed nothing untoward in them and even after a thorough search of the house and surroundings during the days that followed, no clues were found as to who had committed the atrocities. Three children had vanished, and their mother almost beaten to death. The only blessing – if it could be called that – said Scoop, was that her memory never returned.

No amount of turning over the facts led them to any fresh conclusions about what happened, but it was evident to Polly which way Sarah's thoughts were turning when she asked Denny, "Were the house lights on when you picked him up earlier? And when he turned back to the house, saying his wife was calling him, did you hear, or see her?" Denny said he had only seen Elvis and started to say that the lights weren't on then changed his mind. He pointed out that it was still daylight and he wouldn't have noticed, even if they were.

Not being dim, both men saw the implication, but Denny protested... "Oh, come on – let alone what happened to his wife, how could he have spirited away the children without being seen?" Scoop agreed. The neighbours saw him drive home and were adamant that neither his nor any other vehicle passed their property during the afternoon. It was a pleasant day and Arthur Simpson had spent several hours reading in the garden. Someone on foot, Scoop said, could have reached the cottage through the woodland (and a couple of fields) on the other side, out of his sight, but not a vehicle.

Neither Denny nor Scoop had any idea what happened to the dog, but most probably it had been taken to a local kennels, to be adopted. It had not been as obviously a guard dog as the one that was haunting the young family ...which suddenly caused Denny to remember something odd that he had not thought of before. "Whenever I drove Elvis home, he always reminded me to sound my horn when we approached the cottages. It's strange, now that I come to think about it, but, on that night, he didn't. When I pulled up he jumped straight out and ran through the gate. He must have been frantic with worry, seeing all the lights on."

As an afterthought, Sarah asked if Perry still lived in the area and Denny said they had rarely met afterwards. During the week she survived, before slipping into a coma, the poor man spent every hour in the hospital at Mary's bedside.

He was granted leave by his employer and he certainly wasn't drowning his sorrows in *The Grocer's Arms*! He did ring Denny when his wife died and said he intended to move well away from all reminders of this place. "It wouldn't surprise me if he hadn't moved to Spain," Denny volunteered. "He never stopped complaining about the British weather!"

By the time they had talked themselves out, it was almost teatime, but all had enjoyed the afternoon and their guests were happy that, should any more information come to light, they would be informed. Polly insisted on Sarah resting while she cleared up, promising to bring her a cup of tea when she'd finished.

Knowing it was pointless to protest, Sarah was only too glad to put her feet up... It was more than likely that she would not be alone for long.

25. Meanwhile...

During the afternoon, Elly was fascinated to see pictures of many places that stirred her memory. Clarrie had opened the computer program showing newspaper photographs of the house where the child's remains had been found. She explained that the lady who had rescued her brother, Jamie, was Mrs Mace. "Did you ever follow them when they went out," she asked, "to the river, or seaside?"

Elly nodded – then sent her thought waves realising that she could not always be seen by Clarrie, who showed her pictures of other towns and villages. Moving ever closer to the coast, Clarrie slowly concluded that their destination was Formby. They had most likely taken a bus directly from home to the popular beach.

By chance, one of the pictures she clicked on caused Elly to utter a cry of surprise, so she stopped to enlarge it. When the A565 turned away from the coast, Clarrie clicked through a few pictures of the surroundings and Elly suddenly became excited and pointed to a church...

"Granny and Grandpa," she shouted, "they go there! We go now," she demanded.

Clarrie knew that would be a bad move because it was unlikely that the couple would be there – or indeed anywhere now, but it did point to the fact that they had lived in the district. It was consistent with the grandparents, having visited Elly's home somewhere on that coast.

Elly, reminded of the fact that they were following the bus route to the beach where Jamie had been taken from her, was eager to get back to the task and eventually she stopped Clarrie with an excited shout when she recognised an avenue of trees, which after leaving the bus, they had walked along to get to the beach. The last few pictures were of Formby beach and their search seemed complete.

Now all that they had to do was find Elly's home and trust that the shock of finding her parents would not destroy the child. They had yet to convince her that she was no longer eight-years-old.

It was likely that her grandparents, if living, were still near to the church – older people usually needed to be nearer to shops and public transport. She noted the location exactly and would inform Sarah and Alec as soon as possible.

Elly's parents might well have lived within walking distance of Formby: near enough for the grandparents to visit frequently but not close enough to 'drop in'. It was when they were visiting that they took the children for a walk. Clarrie located a picture of Formby Cliffs while Elly was still howling her displeasure at not returning to the Church.

"Tell me about the day Gran and Gramps came to see you; they took you and Jamie for a walk..."

"To see the sea, to give mummy a rest!" interrupted Elly.

"Yes," Clarrie agreed. "Did you walk from your home, or did you ride in a bus or car?" she asked.

"Gran wanted to take Jamie in his pushchair but he wouldn't sit in it – he wanted to walk because he was a big boy – and Grandad said it was alright because he could carry him if he got tired – so Gran agreed but she didn't like it – she told him Jamie was too big to carry and would break his back – which was silly – I know it was silly because Gramps said so." At last Elly stopped to take a breath, by which time Clarrie had found pictures of the cliffs and the town.

She showed Elly, who pointed to the distant sky and said 'sea'. The sea was out of sight, so it was likely that she had been there – and had perhaps lived not far away.

Clarrie wondered if Elly could find her way home from this point but decided not to push her any more for the moment. She also abandoned her original plan to go to the beach where Elly's brother had drifted ashore and she had lost her life.

Before Elly became upset, not getting her own way, Clarrie switched to a game they could play together, and the child was soon happy counting how many Teddy bears she could find in a big picture of a toy store. It was time Sarah attempted to explain to Elly what had happened to her and helped her to accept that her little brother was now a grown man.

When the game ended she left photographs of Jamie revolving on the screen to occupy Elly, while she went to telephone her mother.

When Polly returned to their front room with a laden tea trolley, she caught the tail end of her conversation with Clarrie. She commented that it sounded as if Elly's memories were returning. They are, to a limited extent, Sarah agreed. Now that the child could picture where her grandparents had lived, it was conceivable that she would be drawn there, and goodness only knew what effect that would have.

Before they ate, Sarah rang Alec, so that he could set up a police enquiry into who had been officials and members of the church, twenty years ago. It should now be simple to discover the grandparents' name and that of Elly's family – and where she had lived with her parents.

It was a situation that needed sensitive handling and Alec had already said that when the time came to tell them of Jamie's survival, he would like Sarah to be present. Her thoughts were drawn away from Elly when another visitor began to take shape...

Polly, knowing the signs well, guessed from the way Sarah looked beyond her slightly, her eyes unfocussed, that she should sit quietly and await developments. The television news had just started, so it was not difficult to relax and ignore what might be happening in the same room – confident that she would hear all, later...

When the news bulletin came to an end, Polly saw that Sarah was resting back in her chair seeming half asleep – no longer staring at who knew what... She opened her eyes and smiled when the television volume was turned down. "Well, Polly, I have had a frustrating chat with, I think, Mary's first husband Geoff Bryce. He gets so angry and frustrated when I can't immediately grasp what he is trying to tell me that I have only understood two or three phrases. I tried to ask about the children – his children – and he said, *'You have the photograph,'* and *'Look in it, they are there'*...He finally disappeared, and I am completely confused because we have seen no pictures of his family at all, except for distant shots in Theo's collection."

They were both disappointed that Mary herself had not materialised but accepted the fact that, if she did, it was likely to be with Elly.

"I had no idea that the afterlife would be so conventional about waiting for formal introductions and invitations," Polly said with a grin. "I feel sure that she will come if she's really beginning to feel out of place where she is."

"Let's hope we have more answers for her before then. I wonder if we could ask Theo for another, more organised search through his albums."

"You know he would jump at the chance to entertain us again," Polly smiled, "but all that can wait. You need to get to bed early and sleep late tomorrow."

"Yes *mother*," Sarah replied with a grin, "but I do want to go over our plan so that I can get my head straight before I try to sleep. It will escape me otherwise – sleep will, I mean – I am unlikely to lose the plot but there are now too many loose ends."

Polly took out her notebook and wrote:

1. Elly: Check with Alec – her parents' name and address

2. Ask Barbie, Bill and Mercy if they knew Geoff Bryce

3. Geoff said the children were in a photo – ask Theo

4. If they volunteer to babysit again they might meet Mary

5. What happened to the accident compensation money?

6. Ask Alec about the early searches for the children.

No doubt, the more they encouraged people to talk about the mystery, other points would crop up, but Polly said she would telephone Barbie, Bill and Mercy tomorrow; she would also visit Harry the House and Kevin the Car.

Sam Slater, who still owned the open land and the original farmhouse, had not known the old cottages when occupied. He had demolished them as soon as the land was his, to make room for the estate, many months after Elvis Perry moved out, but he might have known him. He had been kind enough to give them copies of the estate plans, which showed clearly where the labourers' cottages had been so Polly added him to her list. There was no harm in including him in their enquiries.

Sarah would ring Theo about the photo albums and suggest volunteering their babysitting threesome again but otherwise would concentrate on dealing with Elly. It was going to take all her tact and patience to make the child understand what had happened to her.

The morning didn't go entirely as planned. Sarah, having roped Theo into babysitting and bringing all his photos with him, had a call from Alec. It would take hours of her time, but he wanted her to talk to Dora Mace and, when she agreed, said a driver would arrive within the hour to take her to the police station nearest to the hospital where Dora was under guard.

It seemed to Sarah that they didn't quite know how to handle the poor woman, so she promised to do whatever she could. Polly was out, so she wrote a note to explain what had happened and tell her about babysitting again the following night.

It suddenly seemed that everything was happening at once and time running short ...but that was silly, Sarah reflected, as she hurried to prepare herself for what was likely to be the whole day out.

The car arrived five minutes early and Sarah walked out, before the driver had time to reach the front door. He ushered her into the rear seat, hoping she would be comfortable; they were not picking up anyone else and she should please slide the partition if she needed anything.

It was a beautifully sunny day, yet still with a pleasant crispness in the air and she looked forward to travelling through countryside, rather than heavily populated towns. Only after she settled comfortably, and the car was moving away did Sarah realise she was not alone after all. Smiling happily and fidgeting with excitement, Elly asked her, "Now are we going to see Jamie...?"

Sarah smiled, but even so, sighed. It was likely to be a very long day.

26. The End in Sight?

It was almost half-past-one when they reached the local police station and the Superintendent in charge was eager to take Sarah to lunch. He had been briefed by Alec up to a point but didn't quite understand why this elderly civilian was to be handled with VIP treatment and he had to follow whatever she suggested to the letter.

During their meal, her host, Bill, described the scene at Dora's house when he'd arrived. The plumber had made a pot of tea and was shaking, trying to carry a tray into the front room, where Dora Mace and her neighbour were waiting, under the eye of a young policewoman. "The teacups were rattling on the saucers, so I took the tray from him and then left them all waiting there while I went up to the attic. The blanket, still wrapped round the body, was soaked, but there was very little water pooling round it."

"From what I heard," Sarah replied, "it had all leaked into the room below. If it had not been for that, the plumber would never have been called and Mrs Mace might never have been shocked into remembering what she had done with her little boy's body." Bill frowned, and she sensed the normal official mistrust – reluctance to believe that anyone could forget such an act and determination to pursue a kidnapping charge.

"The boy's death was natural, apparently, and his doctor may have intended to have admitted him to hospital, but the poor man was involved in a nasty traffic accident around that time. He and the records he had with him were lost when his car burned out. We are assured that the boy's records on file continued to grow, as did the kidnapped child. There had never been any reason to re-check his blood group or anything else, so his new medic suspected nothing."

On the drive to the facility, where they were holding Dora, Bill was curious about Sarah's involvement. He was helping because he 'owed' Alec and trusted his advice. "I hear that you are acquainted with the family of the kidnapped boy, who is now a young army officer," he probed hopefully.

Sarah couldn't claim to know his parents but said that she had 'met' their daughter. She smiled inwardly, expecting that to put an end to his curiosity, but she was wrong.

"I forgot to tell you, but we've traced his parents. They lost the boy and his sister and had assumed they both drowned. They will be ecstatic if the young woman is also restored to them."

Horrified, Sarah had no choice but to explain. Her dramatic account of Elly's bursting into Clarrie's life, and now hers, stunned Bill into silence and she remained quiet too, worrying what his reaction would be. They had covered at least a mile of country road before he spoke.

"I have to believe that everything you've told me is true – not least because you have obviously impressed

Alec. I understand that you've been of great help with several difficult cases in Berkshire? You've certainly made Alec a believer."

Sarah nodded, and he sighed heavily before speaking again. "I had a great marriage once but it lasted less than eight years. We separated because, after our infant son, died my Bet got involved with Spiritualists, who convinced her that he was still happily growing up beyond the veil. For three years or more she kept pleading with me to believe and to go with her, but I just thought she had gone out of her mind."

Sarah saw that he was nearly in tears but didn't interrupt. "We separated, and I always hoped she would see sense, but we lost touch and five years later I heard from her sister that she had died. I wish I had not been so pig-headed. I must have caused her so much grief – what a fool I've been."

In an instant, Sarah knew that Bet was with them. When, a few minutes later, she did break the silence she spoke quietly. They had reached their destination and the car was parked.

As Bill removed his keys and opened the car door, she touched his arm gently to hold him back. "I'm glad you told me, and I understand that it does take a great leap of faith to believe in an afterlife. You are not alone in needing proof. I hope you will accept that your wife, Bet, is here now and is very relieved to have heard your regrets. Your Billyboy is here too, still little, as you remember him, and he is offering you an orange-coloured bear with its black woolly nose in shreds, and he says you can 'bowo' it Dada, to help you sleep."

Without waiting for his reaction, fearing that it would be emotional, Sarah left the car and started walking to the entrance where another police escort was waiting. He waved toward the Superintendent's car, where Bill was looking at them as he aimed his key to lock it. Before he approached, Bill stared earnestly at Sarah and mouthed 'thank you'.

They didn't have any opportunity to talk in private again until they were on the return journey, during which Bill could not hear enough about the paranormal.

He recalled being upset when their puppy had chewed the bear's nose and his son, Billyboy, their pet name for him, had always called him Dada. There was no way Sarah could have known or made up any part of what she'd told him, and he bitterly regretted his denials and the rift he had caused with his wife... So few years of her life were left and because of him they were not happy ones.

He found little consolation in the assurance that she understood and was not angry with him. Sarah told him that Bet would always hear if he spoke to her in his thoughts and even though it was unlikely that he would hear her reply, he might find consolation and feel supported if he had a problem.

Sarah had done her best to make him feel better and now needed to return home to prepare herself for her meeting with Elly's brother and an even more difficult one with her parents.

Before either of these could take place, she had to convince Elly that she must move on, no longer tied to the earth plane. Just thinking about all that lay in store was exhausting, but she was exhilarated, remembering how far they'd come since Elly had first caught sight of Clarrie sitting in a car outside a haunted house, twenty years ago.

27. Faster than Email

It was very late when Sarah arrived home. Not wanting to spend more time with Bill, she had left him as soon as she could, without appearing to be rude. Having asked the driver to start their return trip earlier than he had expected she invited him to stop somewhere for a meal with her. He'd been happy to cooperate and said he looked forward to driving her again.

Polly was agog to hear about her meeting with Dora but insisted that Sarah should drink her hot chocolate and go straight to bed – they could talk tomorrow.

When Sarah rang Alec the following morning she put the 'phone on speaker and indicated that Polly should stay, so that she would be up to date and Sarah need not repeat everything; she had been with Dora for three hours.

As she was conducted to the ward where Dora was waiting Sarah was aware that, although she couldn't see her, Elly was with her. The child would be disappointed when Jamie was not there too. Dora was not interested in who her visitor was; she asked immediately for Joe – they had promised that he could visit her. Sarah assured her that the young man would come to see her as soon as he could. She had to make the poor woman understand that the little boy she rescued from the sea all those years ago was not hers, so she started by asking for Dora's memories of that day.

"Joe, I need Joe, where is he," cried Dora tearfully.

"I really want to help you, but you need to stay calm and listen to me carefully, while I tell you what I believe happened the day he suddenly became well again – then you can tell me if I have misunderstood." From what she knew of Dora's habits, from Elly, Sarah described the likely scenario that day... "You were so worried about the doctor coming and taking Joe to hospital because your little boy seemed even more ill than usual. You were sure that a day out by the sea would make him better..."

"Yes, that's right," Dora agreed, "The doctor didn't understand... He wanted to take Joe away from me."

"So, you lifted him from his bed, wrapped him safely in his blanket – and then what did you do?"

"We hid in the roof where nobody could find us, then, when it grew dark outside and we were sure the doctor wasn't coming, I left him while I got his pushchair and a little picnic ready so that we would have an early start next day, then I went to bed."

Sarah was relieved that Dora was quite clear up to that point, but upset, having not previously considered that the child could have been left in the attic all night.

No mother would have knowingly done such a thing – then she pulled herself together as Dora continued. "It was really early when I woke the next morning and when I went to his room he wasn't there, so I knew he must be waiting in his chair." Sarah listened patiently as Dora talked, excitedly at first, then growing more hesitant – sometimes starting again from when she'd found Joe's bed empty, until finally she stopped and, sitting up straight and still, she stared wide-eyed into the distance.

The police constable on watch in the corridor glanced briefly through the window shutter, to ensure that all was well, and was surprised to see the two occupants apparently just sitting – one with eyes wide and the other with eyes shut – but it was no concern of his, so he resumed his position with a shrug.

Sarah had been praying for inspiration or help from on high, but forced herself to resume, trying to make it as easy as possible for Dora to accept that she had journeyed to the seaside on her own. "When did you realise that Joe was not in his chair?" she asked.

"When I saw him in the water of course," Dora said… "I only glanced back along the beach for a moment and when I turned, there he was, trying to scramble back to me, so I helped him out. I had to carry him, poor lamb, he was exhausted. There was a girl there – he was trying to get away from her – she must have taken him out of his chair when I wasn't looking."

"No Dora, listen carefully. You misunderstood. That little girl was his sister Elly who was also in trouble, not able to swim. I'm sorry to say that she drowned that day."

Dora was angry and said that Sarah could not possibly know …then she began to shake. "Can you recall what the little boy was wearing? You didn't recognise his clothes, did you?" Again, Dora began to bluster but something had just occurred to her. As soon as they arrived home Joe started asking where Elly was; who was Elly – and who was this woman who seemed to be saying it was her fault that the girl had died?

Deciding that honesty was essential, Sarah tried to encourage Dora to talk as if circumstances were normal and asked her directly if she believed in Life after death and had she ever known anyone who was psychic? Startled by the sudden subject change, Dora blinked and frowned before nodding and saying she had been to a séance once with a friend whose husband had died. With encouragement, she went on to say that the husband spoke to her and said he was well again, suffering no pain and very happy. "It was really so silly, but it made my friend happy."

"How long ago was it?" Sarah asked, "and did you receive any messages yourself"

"Oh, about ten years I think – I can't remember exactly, and I did get a message, but it was even more rubbishy than hers ...telling me that my son loves me and is happy and I mustn't grieve for him. It sounds as if heaven must be full of people who are happy to be dead – but my son wasn't one of them!"

It was the opening Sarah had been hoping for, and with the help of Elly, who was familiar with everything that had happened, she eventually convinced Dora that the message psychic's message from Joe was genuine, and that James' parents had grieved for him for twenty years. They would soon be reunited with him. Sarah was reassuring. "I know he will never lose his love for you. You are the mother he knows best, and he will be coming to visit you soon."

Sarah felt emotionally exhausted when she left, but

Dora finally accepted that she'd made a dreadful mistake and was eager to do anything she could to make up for causing such misery.

Elly was in a forgiving mood too and she had stayed with Dora. When Jamie did come, she said, she would let Sarah know immediately. Sarah smiled, as did Polly when she heard about the child's promise...

"I'll bet she will," said Polly, "she's faster than email!"

28. Priorities

Clarrie was glad that, with Sarah's help, Elly would soon be part of her own family again, but she would miss the child's visits; drawing with her had been fun. Yesterday, Clarrie had shown her photographs of herself taken within a year or two of Elly's passing and, as soon as she saw those of the visit to the haunted house, Elly had pointed excitedly, "That's the girl, there, in the car! She's a bit like you."

"Yes, that *is* me. See how young I was then... If you had still lived in this world you would have grown up too, into a young lady, just as Jamie has grown up into a young man." Clarrie didn't always see Elly, although she always sensed her when she was present. When they 'conversed' it was usually by thought, so on this occasion Clarrie was alarmed to hear Elly crying and even more worried when she realised that the child had gone without warning.

When she rang Sarah to tell her, she was assured that she had done the right thing and Elly would now be forced to accept her position and was better prepared to find her parents. Alec had their address now and was in touch with them. Their son James had been informed but had insisted on seeing Dora again before he met his real parents.

He was devastated to have lost his sister. He had grown up thinking that she was a figment of his imagination ...*she must be if his 'mother' had no idea who he was talking about!*

Thus satisfied, Clarrie could get on with her own life – friends to entertain – paintings to paint – meals to cook – Daxy to doggy-walk – Emma to feed ...in reverse order of importance, of course! Soon, as usual, Daxy's urgent 'woofing' from upstairs informed her that Emma had woken up, so she went to tackle her first happy task of the day.

Yesterday, Del met someone he'd known in Brunei when he was on assignment to cover the expansion of communications. The designer of the solution was Adam Simmons. He'd been invited to come to the office to see the editor, with a view to writing an article. "Writing anything is no trouble to Adam," Del said laughing, "his head is full of statistics!"

Discovering that Adam would only be in the area for a few days and was alone, Clarrie suggested having him round for a meal and inviting Rowena to make up the table. "Fine, as long as you're not matchmaking," Del said, "he might be married for all I know." Clarrie told him not to worry; Rowena was finished with men for life! She had, however seen much more of the world than had Clarrie, so would keep the conversation buzzing.

Having settled the date, she was free to deal with what she still considered to be her work – her art. A recent email from an old college friend had surprised her. They hadn't been in touch for years, but she was writing to give her the URL of her new website. *'Look it* up' she wrote 'and imagine what my designer could do for you. Stevie Mitchell, currently, is a manager with BT but will be setting himself up in the web-design business soon, so get in fast while it's still a hobby!'

Apparently, he was passing within a few miles of her home the following week and had viewed the paintings on her current website. He knew that Clarrie had built it herself and although it worked well, he was excited about the more modern treatment he could give it. He would be happy to call on her, if she liked the idea, and she could contact him directly.

After checking the new website Clarrie didn't hesitate to email Stevie. There was no doubt that her site was sadly out of date and, with that in mind, she spent the rest of the afternoon sorting out photographs of her work into relevant folders. Stevie might not be impressed by her website, but he was not going to find fault with her filing, if she could help it!

Clarrie couldn't remember any day, for weeks, when she had been less haunted and had felt more *normal* but towards bedtime she could not stop her thoughts drifting – wondering with a twinge of guilt how Sarah was coping. Del read her mind, as usual, and urged her to ring up, but she resisted… It was his turn to come first.

29. A Worried Man

So far, Polly's day had gone to plan. Before the driver arrived to whisk Sarah away for another long day, they had rearranged their 'to-do' list. It seemed clear that Mary's first marriage was a happy one, but they needed to be clearer about Perry's circumstances before he became her second husband.

Had he been a family friend?

They decided to rope in Alec for that chore as they had no right to search police records, even if they knew where to look. Sarah suggested that Polly should start with Harry and Kevin as they had known both Mary's husbands (and the area) longer than Mercy, Barbie and Bill. Then she could call on Theo to search his photo collection again, now that they had a better idea about what they were looking for...

The doorbell interrupted them; they hadn't heard the limo draw up. "Luxury VIP treatment again obviously," said Polly with a satisfied smile, "and so it should be," she added as she went to answer it.

A few miles away, a very worried man was fretting about being late for an appointment. The traffic was always heavy at this hour on weekdays; the road had narrowed for the length of the bridge and traffic had to wait until it was clear before starting to cross. Inevitably, sitting in this location forced unwanted memories to the surface.

The rain had been blinding then too – the windscreen wipers couldn't cope – it hadn't been his fault – the wind had blown the boy off his feet and onto the car – it's a wonder the windscreen wasn't cracked. He'd bundled the boy into the car before realising that he was dead, thinking he'd take him to the hospital, but almost immediately realised it was too late for that.

Worried that someone in passing traffic might see him with the body, he slung the schoolbag onto the river bank below. The wind had increased in fury and he couldn't get behind the wheel fast enough. As he drove away he saw the school-cap caught on the screen wiper and visibility was even worse than before. Fortunately, it soon became dislodged and blew off. Relief was now tinged with rage – he should have thrown it into the river with the bag. He wasn't stupid – better that they should think the boy had drowned. rather than know he'd been hit by a car, so he took the body home.

Hiding it successfully was just the beginning and had inspired him to be more ambitious.

He couldn't believe his rotten luck. Until those two busybodies started asking questions, bringing up the 'drowning' again, people had barely remembered what happened. The older one was Polly something – the other seemed to be directing things – and they had now latched onto old Theo, who he used to see often, in *The Grocer's Arms*. He was said to be psychic... *God help me if he is! he thought.*

He knew where Theo lived and in the unlikely event that he was in touch with the afterlife he knew how to deal with him! It would be risky visiting the old pub after all these years but, in addition to aging, he now sported a beard and moustache so was unlikely to be recognised. It was his best chance of keeping up with the local gossip. Tomorrow – yes, he would drop in for a drink. It would be interesting if Theo was there – very interesting!

As Sarah approached the car, her driver was holding open the rear door but, when he saw her hesitate, he asked if she would prefer the front passenger seat.

"I do like to enjoy the view more than is possible from the back, so yes please, but I have no excuse – can't plead car-sickness," Sarah smiled as she accepted his offer. He seemed pleased – they had, after all, had a pleasant meal together and were not complete strangers. Even so, she was glad that conversation was spasmodic. Her mind was fully occupied with the coming meetings, not being entirely sure what to expect.

Fortunately, the driver made no attempt to engage in trivial chatter.

When she did venture to ask about their destination, she discovered that they were heading to the prison hospital again. Alec had told her that, at the request of James, who was devastated to discover that the woman he had grown to love was not his mother, Sarah would accompany him to meet his real parents. The young man was nervous and needed to be clearer about what had befallen the sister who he'd been encouraged to think was a dream and had never existed!

Sarah could imagine how dubious he must be about her connection with Elly and understood that he needed to discuss that aspect before meeting two strangers who were likely to become emotional. She had not expected to meet him when he visited Dora Mace and just hoped that she could bring some sort of comfort to them both.

30. Coming to Terms

The driver passed all the necessary paperwork to the constable awaiting them at the hospital entrance, who then conducted Sarah through reception. Together they walked the long narrow corridor to the lift. The number of locked gates they had to negotiate, all of which entailed standing in wait while paperwork was studied, disconcerted Sarah. She was surprised that Dora was deemed to require such high security but conceded that to the authorities she was a criminal – an unknown quantity.

There was a young army officer standing outside Dora's ward, chatting to the seated constable and as soon as he saw Sarah he stopped abruptly to greet her. After saluting a greeting, he hoped she wouldn't mind his having waited for her before going in. He suddenly looked nervous when he said he didn't know how to introduce himself.

Sarah put him at ease by saying that she had known him as Jamie from the first moment she learned of his existence. "Your sister Elly knows me as Sarah, so that seems the best place to start." Turning to her guide she asked, "Is there somewhere we can talk privately for five minutes please?"

The adjoining ward was unoccupied, and James

waited for Sarah to decide whether to sit on the bed or the chair. She smiled as she chose the chair… "My back needs all the support it can get these days." A peal of giggles greeted this declaration, startling Sarah enough to cause James to ask if she was alright. Mentally asking Elly to sit quietly while she explained to her brother that they were not alone, Sarah saw that Elly was looking doubtful. It was clear that she could not accept that this man was her baby brother. As if in confirmation, Elly asked when Jamie would be here.

Before she could convince them both to accept the other, she needed to revive any memories a three-year-old might have retained into adulthood. Alec had informed James that she was psychic, so it was now up to her to convince him that it was true.

Elly was fidgeting impatiently, with her eyes going constantly to the door. The little brother she knew was not going to come back; Elly must accept that, had she lived, she would also be a grown-up.

"I believe you have memories of your sister Elly. May we please speak of her? She is here and can help if you try."

Looking very doubtful James said he would, but Elly holding his hands and telling him to be a good boy felt like a dream. Whenever he did something he knew was naughty, he said, he could almost hear her shouting '*BAD BOY*'.

"I did, I DID…" Elly screamed. "He pretended he couldn't hear me!"

James remembered being surprised that Elly wasn't with him – he was sure they had been together that morning. He'd asked where she was and was told that he'd been dreaming... There was no Elly. Thinking back now, as an adult, he recalled being pampered – toys, treats – he only had to ask for something and it materialised like magic. He could do no wrong and he was cuddled a lot. It no doubt overcame any doubts he had, and his new life blotted out all that had gone before.

"Jamie wouldn't forget his favourite toy; he can't be Jamie," moaned Elly.

Seeing something to grasp, Sarah asked Elly what his favourite toy had been, and Elly was quick to say that it was a big red bear on wheels that he sat on while she pushed him around the garden. "Elly is with us and she can't believe, if you really are Jamie, how you could have forgotten your favourite toy. She has described it to me. She says it was big and red and on wheels. She used to push her little brother on it."

"Oh, my God," he whispered, "a woolly bear!" The memory had come rushing back and with it were others... We went for walks, always holding hands... Then we were running to look at something and I fell. I don't know whether she fell too but I remember a lot of water and I was frightened."

"I'm afraid Elly was with you in the water but the woman who pulled you out did not rescue Elly." Sarah didn't want to plant any bad feeling towards Dora, so she explained that Dora, who was out of her mind with worry about her child being so ill, had thought he was her own little boy and that Elly was trying to steal him away. James knew about the discovery of Joe's little body and shuddered – visibly upset. Sarah hastily started to discuss his real mother and father, constantly interrupted by Elly who was beginning to believe that he really must be her brother and wanted to talk more about what they did together. "Elly is telling me that you were very skilled at kicking a football,"

"Well, yes, I have always liked kicking a ball about…" He frowned and closed his eyes for a moment, then added, "I can't think what happened to it, but there used to be a net that I could aim for."

Elly was shouting with delight. She said their Daddy had made it for them and he'd painted it yellow. At the same time, James was telling Sarah that the posts were yellow. "I wonder what happened to it."

"It is a memory from your early years with Elly. She says your father made it, but it wasn't a real one and it always fell over when the ball went in."

"That's right," he laughed, "I remember my Elly now – she was the one who had to keep picking it up." James' eyes started to moisten as he suddenly realised that his 'rescue' from drowning had deprived him of so many happy memories. Whatever her motivation and however ill she had been, it was wicked of Dora to abduct him as she did and let Elly drown.

Elly left Sarah's side and climbed onto the bed to sit with James and reached for his hand. As if he had felt her touch he looked down at it and then clasped his hands together.

Sarah smiled. "Elly seems to have accepted that you are her Jamie, so I think it's time we visited Dora. You need not say goodbye to her – perhaps you will want to see her again, but until she faces what she did and is no longer confused, it might be better not to make any promises. The medics will advise you, I'm sure."

Sarah was aware that James was still feeling torn between his attachment to Dora and a burning resentment for what she had done. Elly was singing and feeling excited to be going home. She was aggrieved about the amount of time they were spending with *'that bad lady'* and was happy to see all the bars that were keeping her in prison. She had asked Sarah if they would ever see the little boy who had died … *"Is passing on like being in heaven?"* she'd asked. *"Is he already there?"*

It had not been a pleasant reunion to witness. Dora wanted to hug and hold 'Joe', who was keeping his distance. Sarah did her best to make Dora acknowledge that because she had been worn out and worried when he was a toddler, she had made a terrible mistake. Her little son was ill and would not have lived long, even had he been taken to hospital but Dora's burden, having stolen another woman's child, was enough to bear without thinking her own boy might have lived had she not forgotten where he was, in a cold, draughty attic.

Eventually, Dora accepted that Joe had never recovered and the young man visiting her was on his way to meet his real parents. At that point James approached her and took her hand. Holding it, he said gently, "I will not forget you and we can keep in touch. I will visit you whenever I can." Turning abruptly before she could answer, he left the room. Sarah spent some time with the distressed woman and by the time she left had managed to convince her that her life was not over.

James was obviously not going to abandon her, and his mother might well wish to speak to Dora one day. There must be many moments she could share with the mother who had missed her son's childhood. Sarah could not ignore the grief Dora had inflicted but would do her best to convince Mr and Mrs Deeds that she was not truly evil.

31. Introductions

Two hours later, after a light lunch with the local Police Chief – Elly 'occupying' the front passenger seat – they were on their way to meet James' parents. Their name was not, after all, Hutchinson.

Elly's father had died when she was an infant and although her mother remarried, and she legally adopted by her new daddy, at three-years-old she was already able to say her whole name proudly when asked. Hutchinson was the one she said instinctively, and it certainly caused significant delay when officialdom was searching for her family. So, they were on their way to meet Jean and Robert Deeds.

James perked up enough during the drive to become more curious about Elly. "What is she doing now?" he asked.

"Singing a nursery rhyme …she wants you to guess which one and sing it with her."

"How am I supposed to guess – it's a long time since I was in a nursery!" He paused and smiled… "It's another test. It's probably the oldest one I remember and every time I heard, or sang it, I almost felt three taps on my fingers. Now, I think Elly must have been trying to teach me to count."

"I did, I did!" Elly clapped her hands delightedly and

started to sing. Sarah joined in and nodded to James, who took the hint and sang along. In the rear-view mirror she saw the driver's face. She smiled broadly at him and he grinned back, but didn't join in singing, *Three Blind Mice.*

For most of the trip to Formby they drove along the M6 motorway from home, south of Oxford, so the trip took less than four hours. With nothing much to distract her, Sarah had been able to enjoy watching James come to terms with the fact that his big sister had really existed and had watched him grow up.

He found that he could question her about their life when he was a toddler and the answers he received, through Sarah, brought back memories. He was beginning to feel that he knew his real parents and could imagine how much they had mourned for them both. Sarah hoped that she would be equally successful convincing them that Elly was also coming home.

Jean and Robert were awaiting their arrival anxiously. Jean moved the curtain to look again at the constable who stood at the entrance to their drive. He knew that at least one of the visitors had to face several hours of driving to return home and the house would be easier to pick out if he stood at the gate – thus saving valuable time.

This time he smiled and waved to her, moving to the kerb as the car pulled into the driveway within seconds.

Mr Deeds senior was with them, biting his lip, looking anxious. He had never recovered from the guilt he carried, having not been able to stop the two children from running and falling into the sea. Nothing had ever persuaded him that it was not his fault and he'd become morose – hardly ever smiling again. His wife, their grandma felt equally guilty and mourned with him until she died.

In the ten years since her death, up to a point, he had recovered some of his former good humour. He had sold their house and moved to a small flat within walking distance of his son, Robert; he and Jean welcomed him at any time he felt like dropping in. They would have been happy for him to live with them, but he refused.

Now, he harboured a secret hope that James would join him in the flat. It could be a home address for him even if he worked away from it for most of the time!

While James jumped out from the other side of the car the chauffeur helped Sarah to alight, and the first person she saw was a small, grey-haired lady who came towards the car and gathered Elly up in her arms. The child clung to her joyfully and Sarah was so entranced, watching them, that she didn't immediately respond to the greetings of her hosts. She whispered quickly to James that his grandma and Elly were now united and walked with him to meet his family. They were prepared because Alec had sent them a photograph of him in uniform but his resemblance to Gerald, his grandfather was striking and the hopeful expression in his eyes was typical of the little boy they had lost.

Hugging him, in tears of joy, Jean said, "There is no mistaking your eyes – lighting up as they always did when you heard the words *'ice cream'* from anyone!"

Amidst laughter the family drifted into the house

and Sarah followed. The driver was taking the constable back to the station and Mr Deed would ring him when he was needed for the trip home. There was no sign of Elly and her grandma, but Sarah had no doubt that as soon as they began speaking of her, she would arrive.

Despite all her experience and brushes with the afterlife Sarah could only guess where lost spirits went before they, if they were lucky, eventually went to what people knew as heaven. It was almost as if they drifted in a timeless zone until, sometimes by accident, they were reminded of the life they had lost and started to seek answers, as Elly had.

Her Grandma would make sure that Elly was no longer trapped on the earthly plane, but Sarah didn't doubt that whenever she was in somebody's thoughts, she would not be far away.

She was right.

When they started questioning Jamie about his life with 'that woman' he immediately objected, pointing out that she was ill and had not been responsible for her actions – and she had mothered him lovingly, as Joe, so it was not easy for him to hate her. Robert immediately apologised and put a hand on his shoulder firmly, approvingly, saying that his response was admirable, and they were very proud of him.

Jean nodded and added that they could see that Dora Mace had made an excellent job of bringing him up, so would try not to be bitter. He had to admit that they had every right to resent his kidnapping and went on to explain how his own memories, particularly of his sister, had been lost.

As Sarah had anticipated, Elly joined them. Staring anxiously at her parents, she asked if they really were Mamma and Dada and immediately accepted that they must be …she'd seen the change in Jamie. She was more anxious to know if Sarah had told them that she had done her best to make Jamie come home but he was a bad boy and wouldn't hold her hand.

Although Jean and Robert had been briefed about what to expect of Sarah, they were embarrassed about their disbelief being so obvious. James had obviously been taken in by this woman, but he didn't know that they had been to several psychics since their tragic loss and not one had been able to offer anything other than platitudes…

Jamie took the initiative and brought Sarah into the conversation by saying that he had learned a lot about his earliest days with Dora because Elly had stayed with him in spirit and described to Sarah what she had seen – like the bus journey to her home, when Dora had made him laugh, imitating the cows in a field.

His parents listened patiently, smiling and nodding in appropriate places, and avoiding each other's eyes until Sarah interrupted to tell them how thrilled Elly was to see so many pictures of her with Jamie in their bedroom… "She recognised her toys and has been playing with them but is now worried and very sorry because she can't make them fit back into the trunk."

Not one of the gathering had left the room since their arrival. Together, Jean and Robert left them to look upstairs. Sarah might well have guessed that they would have family photographs on display, but they were stunned when they looked into their spare bedroom, the old nursery, to find the toy-trunk open and the overflow on the floor, beside it.

When Sarah described the elderly woman, who, when they arrived, had embraced Elly and walked away with her, hand in hand, Gerald gasped... "My wife! How wonderful... Thank you so much." Tears rolled down his cheek and he told Sarah that the knowledge that they might one day be together again was a great comfort.

32. Something to Do

Polly decided to bake while alone for the day. Sarah would have had dinner by the time she arrived home but might appreciate a scone or a sausage roll with her bedtime chocolate. Having finished, she enjoyed a light lunch at the kitchen table, where she could savour the warm smell of freshly baked goodies.

Never one to sit idle, she considered what she might do to further their investigation into the haunting. The ghostly hound was more of a problem than Mary but, if Sarah could persuade her to move on, the dog would, hopefully, go with her.

Upstairs, in the office, Polly spread the contents of the most recent folder on the desk and opened her notebook...

It was difficult not to be distracted by the clear view over the fields to the distant town, which seemed to glow in the warm sunlight. She dismissed the sudden temptation to leave the paperwork and read her latest notes...

...Yes – Elly's parents had been traced, after a lead from Del, who had discovered that Elly's father died soon after she was born, and her mother remarried a few years later. They should have been looking for Deeds not Hutchinson.

Her second notation reminded her that she had still to ask Mercy if she and Arthur had known Geoff Bryce, Mary's first husband, so she transferred that to a new list. The third point was what the ghost of Geoff had said when Sarah asked him where the children were. He said,

"You have the photograph. Look in it, they are there". Sarah had fixed a date for them to babysit and arranged for Theo to bring his albums, but it suddenly occurred to her that it would save time and take advantage of the lovely afternoon if she could visit Theo immediately.

Without delay she rang and, luckily, caught him just as he was about to go shopping. Theo was very happy to welcome company rather than go out, and even happier when Polly promised to drive him to town afterwards.

By the time Polly arrived Theo had laid out the tea trolley, complete with biscuits and the kettle was boiling. Guessing that they would need space he had extended his dining table and collected together every album he owned, plus boxes of unsorted photographs.

Polly had brought with her the newspaper pictures and recounted to Theo the points they had covered with Denny and Scoop over lunch. He was intrigued by the possibility that the house lights might have been on since daylight and was quick see that, in that case, Perry's wife could have been beaten by him before he left for the pub!

Denny had neither seen nor heard her when he was outside in the car. That led to the possibility that the children must also have been removed from the house during the day by Elvis Perry, before he was picked up ...but, if so, how, and where had he taken them?

Surely, they must have gone willingly.

All this had scarcely been put into words before and the implication was shocking.

Despite Polly's warning about jumping to conclusions, Theo was now convinced of Elvis Perry's guilt and eager to search the pictures... "But what exactly are we looking for?" he asked. He was open-mouthed, to hear that Sarah had been told by the spirit of Geoff that they must have seen them in a photograph... *Why couldn't he have conversations with the spirits he saw?*

Polly admitted that she was not sure how seeing the children in a photo would tell them where they were now, but until they found the one in question they couldn't guess.

Three hours later they had found only three photographs with the children in view. They were not much more than specks in the distant garden and added nothing to what they already knew. It was disappointing, but Theo said Polly should take them to show Sarah.

He was gathering the loose photos together, but suddenly hesitated and stared at one, not one of the children but a closer view of the dogs in the garden. His slightly glazed look was one Polly recognised... Sarah had moments like that! "Perhaps," he murmured, "we should include all I have of the grounds – back and front."

Polly insisted on clearing the tea trolley and washing up while Theo removed several more pictures from his collection to show to Sarah and readied himself for his shopping trip.

Later, after dropping him in town, ignoring his

protests, Polly told him she would wait for him in the coffee shop; she could study her notes just as easily there as she could at home and, anyway, she had a few phone calls to make.

Polly did make some calls. One was to Mercy Swann, to ask if she had ever known Geoff Bryce. It seemed that she hadn't. She and Arthur had always assumed that Elvis Perry was the children's father. Although it did explain, she said, why he appeared to be less than loving towards them. "It is rather sad," she added, "that during the week before the tragedy he spent hours with them in the garden; I think they were pretending to camp out, or something – they had blankets draped over the fence."

It was disappointing, Polly thought …and yet it seemed a strange way of making a tent. Even so, she noted it in passing.

She was looking forward to hearing how Sarah had coped with her day and hoped she wouldn't be too tired to talk about it. Her own afternoon with Theo was hardly worth reporting – there was nothing new to tell anyway.

When Theo reappeared, it was obvious that he had hurried to avoid keeping Polly waiting so, partly to convince him that the time was not important but mostly because the poor man was breathless, she insisted on treating them both to a hot drink… "One for the road," she joked.

After driving him back and returning home herself it was almost seven-o-clock. She had prepared a casserole in the slow cooker, before going out, so that it could be ready quickly if Sarah arrived early. If not, she would have some for supper herself anyway and it would be fine for their supper the following night.

Polly prided herself on being well organised, which was why she made endless notes – and why she intended to spend the rest of the evening sorting through all her folders to collate the numerous notes she had made about the haunting; who knew what might have been overlooked!

It was quite by chance that he saw the 'Polly-woman' and Theo together as he was driving out of town. They were emerging from a coffee shop and walking to the car park behind it. His business was finished, and the rain had stopped hours ago, so he decided to follow them. He could not have explained why? Curiosity, he supposed.

Were they a couple perhaps?

No. Thirty-minutes later she had dropped him off at his home and returned to her own. There was nobody already inside – he could tell by the way the indoor lights came on ...including the porch light, so the other woman was expected. The trees lining the road might shield him from the view of the windows, but his presence would look suspicious to anyone going into the wide driveway.

There were no near neighbours, so he could not be thought to be calling on anyone else. Reluctantly he decided to leave, but now he knew where they lived too... They would do well not to poke their noses any deeper into his business.

From the first-floor office window as she drew the curtains, Polly saw the car pulling away. It had been there long enough for her to worry about why the driver had parked outside.

It was the car that had seemed to be following her and had it not moved she'd intended to ring the police. Before she forgot, she recorded in her notebook what she could remember about the car.

33. Last Drinks

It was approaching her normal bedtime when Polly heard the car crunch into the gravel drive. She had intended waiting up at least another two hours although, by then, it would be obvious that Sarah must be staying away overnight – and she would be sure to telephone anyway.

Earlier, the television hadn't interested her, and the sound was low, allowing her to hear approaching traffic but, after walking several times to the window only to be disappointed, she now sat where she could see the driveway through a crack in the curtains. Spreading Theo's photographs on the wide window sill, she soon became absorbed in comparing shots of the farm with each other. The press photos were blown up, showing more detail but, strangely, none of Theo's was a match to any...

Just as Polly was identifying the problem, headlights flashed, and the car pulled into the drive.

Photos forgotten, she hurried to open the door, relieved that Sarah was safely home again.

Although tired, Sarah couldn't disappoint Polly, so she just stayed up long enough to describe the reactions of Elly's parents, not only to seeing their son again, but eventually accepting that Elly was with him!

They had a light supper and took hot chocolate to bed with them – it was obviously not the best time for Polly to describe her own day – that could wait until tomorrow when they would both have benefited from a good night's sleep.

When he'd glanced around the pub on arrival, several hours ago, he had seen no familiar faces. Realising that twenty-odd years would have changed everyone, as much as they had him, he studied the occupants more carefully.

The Grocer's Arms was still the most popular drinking spot locally and a couple of old men were vaguely familiar ...facial changes were probably fewer between sixty and eighty – just more wrinkles, plus shrinkage! For an hour or two he hid behind a newspaper, avoiding getting into conversation and observed several men who, contrary to his expectations showed no sign that they remembered him.

Feeling at ease, finally, he went to the bar for a last drink just before ten-o-clock and saw several people he hadn't noticed before. The dartboard hung on the back wall, where the bar curved away from the main seating area and a game was in progress. While he stood, sipping his beer, someone tapped his shoulder... "Good heavens! It *is* you, isn't it? – Long-time no see!" He turned, shook hands and forced a smile. "I hope you're not leaving yet – we have a lot of catching up to do."

It was the last person he would have wanted to meet but there was little he could do, so he sat with a smile and, after glancing at his watch, claimed to have only five minutes but said he could return tomorrow night if nine-thirty wasn't too late? It was a date, they agreed.

As he left he was thoroughly shaken, realising the gist of the 'catching up' he was likely to face if he did turn up, but what else could he do?

Not wanting to go home, where his wife and sister-in-law would be watching the telly, he parked his car out of sight, a short walk away from the nosy-parkers' house, which was still lit up inside.

The porch light was off.

So, the other woman must be home now, he thought. Crouching outside, he could see enough to guess they were sitting, talking happily, having a bedtime snack. He wasn't quite sure why he had returned to spy on them at this hour, but after the disturbing encounter with his 'old friend' his mind was whirling, and he couldn't face going straight home. He had already sensed that they were a threat and was now convinced. He needed to discover all he could about why they were poking about in his past.

His view of the room through the small gap in the drapes was limited, so it wasn't long before his eyes fell to the photographs scattered on the window sill. They were all familiar to him and he clenched his fists in fury. Those that had appeared in the newspapers were large and easy to see but from what he could tell, the others were also of his cottage garden. There was no point in staying longer – it was clear that he was under investigation, but they were not the police. He badly needed to know why, and he knew who to ask.

34. Too Late for Bed

Despite her exhaustion the night before, Sarah was sitting at the office desk checking emails before nine-thirty, sipping a cup of coffee that Polly had just brought up to her. Glancing through her incoming mail, she was surprised to see one from Denny Davies. It was the last to download last night and after saying it was past his bedtime, he said he would be visiting her in the morning – lots to tell her urgently – ring him if not convenient...

Having been warned that they were expecting a visitor, Polly made a batch of sausage rolls and a sandwich cake. She filled it with jam and cream and covered it with chocolate, remembering that Denny had a sweet tooth.

They were both eager to hear what he had to tell them and watched the clock anxiously as the hours passed. Sarah was suddenly distracted by the appearance of Elly at her side... The child was pulling excitedly at her sleeve and pointing at the telephone. *"Jamie, Jamie,"* she screamed with delight. Sure enough, it had started ringing – but it rang on the kitchen extension too and was picked up by Polly.

Not understanding, Elly howled with frustration, but Sarah picked up the receiver anyway and said, "Jamie, for me I think. Thanks Polly..."

The first thing Jamie said was, "Wow, I know you are psychic – but –" ...Sarah laughed.

"I have to confess that a very excited young lady came to tell me!"

Jamie was ringing to thank Sarah for all she had done to reunite his family. He was amused to hear that Elly had forestalled his surprise call and said he would have to think twice before he did anything in future in case the child's eyes were on him! "So, Elly can read my mind too," he said. "That's a thought that doesn't thrill me, I must say!"

Sarah could see his point, but assured him that in a very short time, Elly would come to understand that she was also a grown up and there would be far more to learn and enjoy. Her visits to him were likely to be limited to the moments when he thought of her.

Somewhat reassured, Jamie admitted that, in any case, he was very happy to have her back; there had always seemed to be something missing in his life, no matter how much attention he had received and how many toys.

He made sure that Sarah could contact him if ever Elly had a message for him and they exchanged email addresses.

Polly joined Sarah when her call ended and after being brought up to date – started chuckling again, recalling her confusion when Sarah knew who was calling when she hadn't even had time to find out herself. "It's a pity Elly couldn't monitor all our calls so that we could avoid picking up those we don't want."

"Speaking of calls – do you think Denny might have

tried to call? The morning has gone now, and he sounded so eager to give us his news that I expected him hours ago." They agreed that it would be an idea to ring him but there was no answer. "Do we know any of his neighbours, or friends, who might know where he is?" Sarah wondered anxiously.

She agreed that they should go ahead with a light lunch that he could share if he arrived soon; she knew how Polly fretted about her eating meals on time, so it was better to fall in with her tentative suggestion.

The afternoon became evening and there was still no sign of Denny. His phone was not being answered so they were both worried, but unsure who to inform. Eventually, Polly volunteered to ring the local newspaper office to speak to Scoop. It was not like calling the police, which surely would be a bit 'over the top' but would have the same effect ...Scoop would be eager to help.

It was just after ten-o-clock when Scoop's final call came. It was the third since his search had begun and he said there was no alternative to calling the police; Denny was definitely missing.

They were close friends and had keys to each other's home, so when there was still no answer to the doorbell Scoop had let himself in.

The morning paper was still on the mat and Scoop made his way upstairs, wondering if he would find his friend asleep, or ill. There was no sign of his having slept in the bed, so it was possible that he had telephoned Sarah from a public box and stayed out – but she was sure that he'd been about to go to bed; he kept strictly to his regular bedtime and liked to be up early.

If he had risen early today to go out, Scoop knew he would not have re-made his bed immediately; he would have thrown the covers back to air. He would also have picked up the paper to read over his breakfast. It was therefore clear that something untoward had happened very soon after he'd called Sarah. After a quick look around, he found Sarah's phone number scribbled on a scrap of paper on the floor under the bedside table where the telephone stood.

As Sarah surmised, he had rung before going to bed...

What had happened to stop him? Could someone have called on him – and if they had, would he have gone down to answer the door? It was then that Scoop felt a draught and noticed the unfastened window on the side of the bay. Perhaps the note had been blown off the table. When he looked out he saw that it overlooked the front entrance, so, if he was right, Denny had opened it, recognised his caller and gone down to let him in.

In the last three hours, Scoop had visited every place Denny might be and enlisted the help of other friends.

Nobody had seen him since he'd been in *The Grocer's Arms* the night before. He had left alone...

After reporting to Sarah, Scoop rang all local hospitals in case Denny had been admitted and then went in person to the police station to speak to a mate of his. Detective Sergeant Nick Evans knew him well enough to believe that there was something seriously wrong and promised to act immediately. A general 'lookout' alert was in place within the hour but by dawn the following day it was made an official search for a missing person and the area of interest was extended.

Denny's car was still in the drive, so wherever he went, if not within walking distance (already ruled out) he had been taken as a passenger. When forensics reported that there was evidence of a scuffle, and perhaps someone falling against the hall table, it raised the possibility that he had not left willingly.

They were both worried, but Polly couldn't help saying that Sarah would surely *know* if anything awful had happened... Sarah was touched by her faith but slightly irritated; it sounded as if, due to her inadequacy, Denny could be in trouble! When those in spirit spoke to her, it was never at her instigation, but there was no harm in shutting her eyes and sitting quietly for a while – making herself receptive. Polly recognised the signs and left the room with an understanding nod.

After a while, Sarah gave up. She did try to concentrate on Denny, but her thoughts kept drifting back to the photographs that Scoop and Theo had given them. It wasn't an encouraging sign that she felt unusually cold and at last she became convinced that Denny would not be found soon.

Why couldn't she just shut up... Elvis Perry was sick of having to explain his every move – his wife was worse than ever, having her sister to back her up. *"It was well after three when you came home, Elvie,"* Shirley had chipped in. He was well aware of the time and had let himself in as quietly as he could... He had even managed to climb into bed without disturbing Ellen.

Now she was nagging him too.

He explained again that an old mate's car had broken down and he'd taken him home – then stayed for a cup of hot chocolate that was on offer. It was a good story and he didn't know why they were finding it difficult to accept.

On returning to the pub, he'd seen Denny's car still parked so he waited out of sight for him to leave, knowing that Denny was unlikely to be long.

In fact, he appeared within minutes and headed for the car park. Having caught him up, he had a revealing five minutes with him before Denny insisted that he needed his beauty sleep and would see him tomorrow!

"We've been chatting it over" he'd said, *"and there are some puzzling things about the night your wife was attacked, but I'm sure you can explain."*

'*We*', apparently, included the two woman whose interest, according to Denny, stemmed from their investigation into a haunted house.

It must be the one he'd already heard about – the gossip machine was working overtime. It was bizarre that they had decided that the thing haunting the place was the ghost of his first wife! God only knew where the speculation would lead – especially if they enlisted Denny's help.

As he watched Denny pull out of the car park, he realised that their conversation would be reported back to the two women. He was thoroughly shaken by Denny's demeanour, which had changed, as if seeing him in a new light. He couldn't risk the idiot talking to anyone else.

Before Denny's car was out of sight, he was behind the wheel of his own, following. One thing was certain, he and his wife would be going back home tomorrow – he'd had enough of this place.

35. Three Long Days

As the first day of Denny's absence drew to a close, a full-scale search was underway and there had been no sign of him anywhere.

Just before dinner, Polly had a phone call from Gavin. He had seen the newspaper report and wondered whether he should call the police. Apparently, he and Dave were in the local, playing darts on the night Denny disappeared and had seen him leave. "Yes, he left alone, but earlier he was chatting to a guy I feel I know... There was something about him – something about seeing them together – that seemed familiar.

Polly buzzed for Sarah to pick up the 'phone and, having heard Gavin's account, she remembered something Denny had said when he and Scoop visited them ...he'd said that he usually gave Perry a lift to the pub and back because, personally, he wasn't much of a drinker and Elvis was!

She asked if the stranger could have been the man whose children were kidnapped from the farm – so, possibly, the husband of Dave's ghost? It had been a wild guess, but Sarah knew that Geoff Bryce was suddenly with her and felt his surge of approval.

She urged Gavin to contact the police if he suspected that the man with Denny had been Elvis Perry.

After the call, Sarah told Polly that she was sure it was Perry, now sporting a full beard and heavy moustache, with longer hair too, he was probably surprised to be recognised. "It does sound as if he's trying to disguise his identity," Polly agreed. "Perhaps that's understandable. The Press, and everyone else he ever knew here, must want to reap up the case, which was never solved."

The spirit of Geoff, for the first time, appeared to Sarah without a trace of anger. He smiled and looked pointedly at the loose photographs and albums, which he had wanted them to see. "It's as if Mr Bryce feels it's all over now," Sarah said quietly.

"For goodness sake," exclaimed Polly, "he's in a perfect position to know everything, including where his children grew up and where they are now... Why can't he just tell us?" When Sarah didn't deign to reply, apart from sighing and shaking her head, Polly returned to the kitchen to check their meal and Sarah picked up the 'phone. It might be a good time to catch Alec, to bring him up to date. As Detective Chief Superintendent of a different division, he might not be in the loop.

After their conversation, he said he would look up records of all attempts to find the three children.

At the end of the second day of his disappearance, there had still been no trace of Denny and the local paper again reported his absence from home, asking for any sighting of him to be reported to the police. This time, alongside the telephone number to ring there was a photograph, which, although taken years earlier, was still a clear enough likeness. Sarah stared at it and tried to leave herself open to receive any message of hope. Nothing came through to her, but, on the other hand, she didn't feel that hoping was pointless.

All they had to do was send out their positive thoughts to him and have patience.

Ellen Perry had always dismissed every reason Elvis put forward to return home. She enjoyed being with her sister and helping her to settle into her new house.

Although older, Shirley had married only recently, so she valued having a second opinion about furnishing and fittings. Whilst recovering from a recent operation she appreciated having her sister helping around the house. Ellen hated feeling that Shirley might well become withdrawn when they left so she introduced herself to as many neighbours as possible – inviting them for coffee or asking their advice about refuse collections and other mundane things.

Within a few weeks it had become evident that Shirley was now accepted and known to half the street; being included in the exchange of gossip was a hopeful sign.

It was by sheer chance that Elvis, on his way out and about to push wide the open door to their sitting room, heard someone say that the Fletcher house was haunted. In an excited, shaky whisper, their guest confided, "Poor Peggy is terrified but her husband, Pete, has called in a friend to get rid of the ghost and is quite sure it will be over soon."

There was a chorus of questions and the woman answered... "Yes, they have three children and theirs is the house on the corner near the end of this road. It's where the old cottages used to be, so they think it's the ghost of the woman who was attacked who haunts the place – who thinks that their three children are hers, because they see and talk to her. How about that!"

His thoughts in a whirl, he made his apologies and wished everyone a nice day. Outside, he abandoned his plan to drive into town and, instead, walked to the end of the street to view the haunted property. Not wanting to call attention to himself, he walked slowly around the corner and climbed over a stile into the field beyond.

After walking farther and viewing from different standpoints, he was convinced that the Fletchers' house covered the same ground as had half the cottage compound.

He stared, fascinated at the corner where the dogs had been tethered. This and its semi-detached neighbour, comprised the whole area that had been fenced off from open farmland. To the right of the Fletchers' neighbour was a wooden fence; it was there that he had hung the blankets – a pretend tent for the children to play at camping. How they had enjoyed themselves... He shuddered and tried to close his mind to the hours he had spent keeping them occupied while Mary was sleeping. She couldn't understand why she was so tired!

He had never believed in ghosts but if the children could see and hear the ghostly woman, there might be some truth in it. His wife would certainly have cause to haunt this spot. How he would love to get inside the house and see for himself, but would he see anything?

And if her ghost saw him, would she recognise him? If she did, would it matter?

Suddenly realising how ridiculous he was being, he turned and walked back to his car. He saw a few curtains twitch as he drove away and cursed the fact that he hadn't shaved after being seen in the pub. The sooner he did so the better – because as things had worked out, his wife's insistence on staying with Shirley, away from home, was playing into his hands, giving him more time to get the truth out of his temporary guest!

He would allow himself just one more day to get him to talk but there was just a chance that the blow on his head had caused permanent damage – in which case, how likely was it that he would ever remember anything?

It would be a terrible risk to kill him – hiding the body would not be easy. If only he could be sure Denny still regarded him as a friend, he could let him live.

Just one more day then.

Decision time!

36. Square One

On the day of Denny's disappearance, because all the news from anywhere passed through Del's office, one of his eagle-eyed staff telephoned him while he was still enjoying breakfast. Knowing that Del's wife used to live within a mile or two of the man who was missing, he thought Del might wish to tell her about somebody called Denny Davies.

Clarrie was shocked, knowing that Denny was her mother's friend, and rang Sarah straight away. Sarah was surprised that the news had broken so quickly and could only hope that he would be found soon. She was unable to suggest any reason for anyone to wish him harm and was hoping he would be found soon.

Sarah obviously didn't want to talk about it, so Clarrie changed the subject. "You'll never guess what Elly wants me to do... I hadn't heard from her for days, but she's wants her parents to see how we found them – so I have to invite them here, together with Jamie, to show them all the sketches and maps – and the photos... Unbelievable! She's getting very bossy."

"Well, she can't talk to them herself, can she?" Sarah could understand the child's frustration – then a thought struck her. Now that Elly understood she was not really eight years old she must feel different. "Have you noticed any change in Elly since she was restored to her family?"

Clarrie reminded Sarah that she could hear, but not always see, the spirits that came to her, but thinking about it now, she was sure that Elly communicated more fluently. "You might well see a change in her, mother. You always told me that babies and children do continue to learn and grow in spirit."

The call ended without Clarrie saying what, if anything, she intended to do about inviting everyone round for a chat, but Sarah was cheered. For a few minutes she hadn't been worried about Denny.

Perhaps being distracted had blocked other communications because Geoff Bryce appeared, smiling. Somehow, she felt he was telling her that all was well, so don't fret. It was with a lighter heart that she went to the kitchen to join Polly for breakfast.

The local evening paper reported that the missing man was still missing, and the police were asking anyone who had spoken with him in the local to come forward. Just before he left, Mr Davies had been seen talking with a bearded man who was not a regular in the bar.

He now regretted not going out as usual even if not for a drink, because Shirley had read the item and, naturally, had shown it to Ellen. Now, his wife wouldn't let it drop.

"It was you drinking with him, wasn't it? Denny Davies was the guy who drove you home all those years ago, when you found Mary, wasn't he? What are you going to do?" Scarcely pausing for breath, she proceeded to tell him... "Go to the police at once. You might be able to help them."

"He was still in the pub when I left, so I can't tell them anything that they don't already know – for God's sake, shut up woman!"

With a glare that could have killed, and uttering not one more word, his wife left the room to join her sister in the kitchen. There was no way he could go to the pub again but, as she was unlikely to question him later, he could go home and check on Denny. He had to discover all that he'd shared with those two women and plan how to get rid of them too.

Perhaps Denny had realised he was being followed the other night, because he'd raced home and, without garaging the car, was letting himself into the house by the time Elvis turned into the drive. Shouting that he was in no mood to talk and would see him tomorrow, he slammed the door.

The bedroom light came on almost immediately, so he had rung the bell and thrown stones at the window until it opened. "Alright," he said, "I'll come back at about eleven tomorrow morning, but I'm desperate for the bathroom now. Please let me in..."

Without preamble, when Denny came down, he'd been silenced with a handy rock and driven twenty miles away to Perry's own empty house. It was well away from nosey neighbours and not even the postman had any reason to go through the locked gate, where the letterbox hung.

Two of Ellen's sleeping powders in warm water, solicitously administered while Denny was still semi-conscious, would wear off soon so he'd need another dose tonight, even though he was in a locked cellar. The sleeping powders were only a temporary solution; when he had coughed up all he knew or surmised, he'd be quietened for ever.

The problem was – he didn't know where to start when questioning him. Denny must have been satisfied at the time that Mary had been attacked and left for dead by an intruder, who had then removed the children.

What had happened recently to change his mind?

Perhaps it was those two women who had put ideas into his head – but they weren't here when it happened, so who could have said anything to them to arouse suspicion?

The couple who were housekeepers for Arthur Simpson might have blabbed about suspecting him – but why ever should they have suspected him? He had been careful to hide everything he did from their view... There was nothing he could do about them anyway – it would certainly set them thinking if he made contact with them on any pretext. His one chance of finding out was with Denny – he had to persevere, questioning him. It was one big headache he could have done without.

Who would have thought that having succeeded in allaying suspicion all those years ago, the case was likely to be reopened ...and all because of a ghost that wouldn't rest!

37. A Nice Drive Out

Sarah and Polly were deeply worried about Denny's disappearance. Because of their connection to Scoop, they knew the police had made no progress in their search but, better still, Sarah now had her own access to the local constabulary. She didn't know how Alec had managed it but, as Chief Superintendent, he'd arranged to have Terry Whitelow temporarily attached to the local force.

Since they last met, Terry had risen in rank from Detective Sergeant to Detective Inspector and as DI, he had welcomed the chance to work with Sarah again.

Terry was fascinated when he heard how much Sarah and Polly had discovered about events at the long-gone farm cottages and, knowing her past triumphs, had no hesitation in believing that Mary Perry was haunting the site where she had once lived. He was lodging with them so when he arrived in time for dinner they invited Theo to join them as he had known Mary.

Afterwards, over coffee, sitting comfortably, they showed Terry their collection of photographs. Perhaps he'd see something they'd missed, to explain Geoff Bryce's words about the children being in one.

After Terry examined every scene showing the garden from all angles he selected two and laid them on the table. Like them, he had seen no glimpse of children at play in the whole collection. "Are you sure, Sarah, that their father said there was a photo of them? What were his exact words."

After a few moments of concentration, Sarah replied. "His exact words were *'look at the photo, they are in it...'* and he was so angry with me that I couldn't hold onto his image..." Staring at the photograph Terry was holding, Sarah suddenly realised her mistake. "Why, of course... *'IT'* was the well! But this is one of Theo's photos; there is no well in the *'scene of crime'* pictures."

"The cottages had been on mains water for at least a year before that night," Theo commented.

Polly, at Sarah's suggestion, Rang Barbie Ball and asked if she remembered seeing a well behind the cottages. She did and was astonished when Polly said that it was not in any photographs taken on the fatal night. Barbie could hardly believe it and said the photos must have been taken from a different angle. She added that it was certainly there when, a few days earlier, the children were 'camping' under blankets tied to the fence! They all stared at each other ...all realising that the same explanation was forming in their heads.

None wanted to voice the thought and eagerly fell in with Terry's suggestion that it was time they took him out for the promised drive, to show him where all these events occurred.

If Denny were to be found Terry needed to become more familiar with the area, and they could carry on speculating about Perry just as well in the car.

When Terry admitted to being a poor passenger, Polly had no objections to giving up the driving seat; she wasn't sorry, not accustomed to the car carrying so much weight she wasn't sure how she would cope.

The car wasn't spacious but they all managed to fit in, with Theo in the front passenger seat, as he knew more about the historical layout of the places they wished to see. Terry drove first to the farmhouse site so that he could see the back of the estate and appreciate how much of the labourers' cottages would have been visible from there. He had a clear view of the haunted house and, with Theo's help, estimated that the old well must once have stood beyond what was now the rear garden, at the side of the Fletchers' house, very close to the waste land that gave access to the field from the estate road.

Theo assured Terry that because of heavy woodland the cottages were not visible from the main road. There were trees bordering all sides of the farm property; the cottages were built where they were so the well could be sited over an underground stream. The track that went beyond the Farmhouse had only led to the cottages and it was now overgrown.

They all agreed that, however unlikely, Elvis Perry might well have murdered his wife, but Theo pointed out that she lingered for a week or two and he hardly left her bedside until she went into a coma. Polly, in turn, pointed out that every time she woke up she screamed non-stop.

Could it have been because the first person she saw was Perry?

"When she quietened down," said Theo, "her mind had been so affected by the trauma that they moved her to the Rest Home, where I was on night duty." He glanced at Sarah and shook his head slightly – he obviously didn't want her to tell Terry that he had seen her in spirit.

"If he did beat her, he must have done it earlier that night, before his friend, arrived," Terry said, "...the friend who is now missing. From what you said about Denny having something important to tell you, Perry, who was with him in *The Grocer's Arms* that night, might suspect that Denny's memory has been awakened by whatever they were discussing or something he saw. Suspecting the significance, he might well have acted quickly to keep him quiet."

"I can't believe he would kill him though, before discovering whether or not he told anyone else," Theo said. They all looked pointedly at Sarah, who shook her head, knowing what they expected.

"The most positive thing to say, is that I have seen no sign of his passing on."

It was enough for DI Whitelow.

If Sarah hasn't seen him, Davies is definitely in the land of the living ...but for how much longer?

As the Fletcher house was nearer, Terry drove back towards the main road and turned left off Farm Lane to view the property from the front. There was nothing of interest to see; the patch of garden where the well had stood was grassed over.

From his sister-in-law's front room, Elvis Perry had heard the car pass by. It was normally a quiet road and, hearing it turn around, he couldn't resist going to the window to check the occupants.

He might have guessed!

The busybodies with two men.

One was Theo Penn – he didn't know the driver and that worried him.

Without wasting time, he dashed to get his own car out. He had to follow; *he had to know what they were up to...*

On their way to Denny's house, to which Terry had a key, Theo pointed out good eating spots and twenty-four-hour shopping places and, of particular interest, *The Grocer's Arms*.

On the edge of town Terry suddenly gave the briefest of warnings to hold tight and, braking sharply, he spun left into a side street. Within seconds he reversed into another side street and parked, several car-lengths from the corner.

His three astonished passengers did as he instructed and crouched lower in their seats.

Within minutes a car passed the junction and Terry smiled. "I suspected we were being followed and can guess by whom: Mr Perry himself I think!"

"It was," Theo agreed, "I couldn't resist peeping..."

Laughing, Terry hastened to get the car back onto their route. "We should be well on our way before he realises he's lost us."

They were soon out of town, passing the road that led to Sarah's house – and within a few miles they pulled into the drive of Denny's cottage, where his car still stood. It looked out of place somehow and Polly said it was so badly parked – could he have been in a hurry to get inside the house? "He might have been frightened by someone following him."

"We'll go inside and check but, according to his and your friend, Scoop, who reported him missing, Mr Davies' bed was not slept in and his morning paper was on the doormat."

When they checked the front bedroom, Terry reminded them that the side window of the bay had been open, so he could have spoken to his pursuer and been persuaded to let him in. "Don't forget that the hall table was knocked over, so he was most likely attacked as soon as the door was opened."

"Nothing would persuade me to let in someone I was afraid of," Theo declared.

Sarah wondered if they were wrong in supposing Denny was frightened. "Perhaps he just didn't want to be bothered ...he wanted to go to bed. They were, after all, old friends. He might have wanted to clear things up – but not when he was so tired."

"Although I take your point Sarah," said Terry, "let's assume the worst of Perry. If he killed his wife and was evil enough to dispose of three innocent children, as we all suspect – even though we haven't spoken our thoughts aloud – then he would go to any lengths to discover what, if anything, Denny suspected and whether or not he had told anyone else."

Polly gasped, horrified. "If he's been spying on Denny, he'll know we are friends and will come after Sarah!"

Theo, who had been listening but not joining the discussion, suddenly whispered to Sarah, "It's Mary, I'm sure she is here. I can smell the clinical odour of the nursing home where she died."

Sarah walked out onto the landing and saw Mary. Her spiritual form wavered as she looked up and spoke from the hallway. "Where is he? Where are my babies?"

"He is with Denny, your friend. Please, help us to find Denny." She didn't know where the idea came from, but it suddenly inspired Sarah to do something she had rarely done before – she cast her thoughts out to Geoff Bryce. His wife needed him. He would understand that Denny was in danger and find a way of saving him, she was sure.

After a brief look through the house and garden – it had after all been searched already by experts – Terry led the way back to the car. "No sign of Perry, by the way," he voiced his thoughts aloud. "He followed us from Farm Lane estate. He must have seen us from inside one of the houses. Does he live on that road?" He asked Theo, who had no idea. He thought it unlikely and said that after his wife's death, Perry had moved away and remarried less than a year later.

Before driving off, Terry made an official call and asked for a search to be made for the current address of Elvis Perry who, between twenty and thirty years ago had resided in one of the farm cottages.

If Denny still lived he must be well hidden and they had to start their search somewhere. If Elvis Perry's property was in the middle of a quiet terrace they could rule it out and move on... If isolated, it would be worth a search warrant.

He asked his passengers if they would allow him to

take them for an early evening meal, now, to save Polly cooking again and, as he was a stranger to the area, where would they like to eat?

Despite a few half-hearted protestations they were all pleased to be relaxing together instead of parting company, and happily accepted.

It was almost ten-thirty when, having taken Theo home, Polly's car pulled into their own driveway. The grinding noise of the overhead garage-door opening woke him from a fitful sleep. Elvis Perry had been waiting for hours for the two women to return ...where had they been all day.

There must be an internal door into the house because the door rolled down again, and lights switched on, upstairs and down. He caught only a fleeting glimpse of the sitting-room before the curtains were drawn.

He'd had time to think while waiting and decided that as well as anything he could get from Denny, he must discover more about these two interfering old women.

Tomorrow, Denny had to talk. He couldn't risk drawing more attention to himself by acting hastily. It was with a renewed sense of purpose that he steered his car out of concealment from the woodland opposite the house. Time to face up to the same old nagging... *'Where have you been all day? You said you'd check that leak in the bathroom... Did you get the shopping we need? Are you seeing another woman...'* the last question accompanied by a derisive laugh, as if there was fat chance of that!

Sighing deeply, he pointed the car in the direction of *The Grocer's Arms* – with luck, he might be in time for a last drink...

38. A Friendly Chat

A night's sleep had not diminished his fury. Elvis Perry was still consumed with anger. That was a neat trick – luring him down a side road – although he wasn't sure how the car had disappeared. It was a quiet road and the damn thing was nowhere in sight! He couldn't believe they knew who he was; he had shaved off his beard and trimmed his moustache, which were drawing too many glances.

He was now on his way, so he'd told his wife, to check up on their own property and make sure the mailbox wasn't overflowing with flyers. Letters were being forwarded, but the box had to be checked; they didn't want it to shout 'Nobody Home' to any passing crook.

He told Ellen not to make dinner for him – he'd stop to eat and have a beer somewhere. He had not missed her eye-roll as he turned away! He made a few stops in town to pick up some extra strong sleeping pills plus food and drink for his 'guest' and fulfil Ellen's shopping list.

Denny was still drowsy when Elvis let himself into the cellar. The days he had been held there had all passed without lifting the fog from his brain. He seemed not to remember the blow on the head, although he did say it ached. He accepted the beer Elvis produced and watched as the pack was stacked alongside another holding water... "In case you get thirsty," said Elvis.

At last, Denny's memory was struggling to come back, and he asked, "Where are we? Why did you follow me home? What time is it – I need to get to bed – I'll talk to you tomorrow." Improvising quickly, Elvis said that he had rescued Denny from the thugs who were following him, and it would be better not to go back home yet, as his place was being watched.

While Denny still looked bemused, Elvis opened a packet of sandwiches on top of a trunk alongside a bottle of water. At first, Denny picked at them dubiously, but soon seemed to realise that he was hungry and finished them eagerly, washing them down with water.

"I'd like to go home now – I'm so tired," Denny whispered. "What did you mean by thugs?"

"They are really after your two friends – the two women who think my deceased wife is haunting a neighbour of Ellen's sister, Shirley. We are staying with her, as I told you, and the street is alive with gossip."

"You mean Sarah and Polly ...lovely ladies. Oh my God – we must let them know they're in danger." Denny struggled to stand but he was still shaky. Elvis consoled him by saying he had taken care of that – not to worry – and went on to ask why they were interested in such an old case as his wife's attack.

Denny frowned and shook his head, obviously he was not in a fit shape to hold a conversation. For over an hour Elvis tried to fish for answers about what the nosey pair suspected, and why, but Denny was not coherent and wanted to know more about the thugs...

Who are they? Where did they come from?

Eventually, glancing at his watch, Elvis decided he'd have to give him another strong powder to keep him quiet until tomorrow night. With foresight, he had brought down a couple of glasses from upstairs and while Denny staggered to the washroom, he opened a beer each; into Denny's he slipped the contents of one packet. When he staggered back, Denny seemed to have recovered slightly and was full of questions. "Why did you bring me here? Who are these thugs? Have you called the police...?"

"Sit down and have a drink and I'll try to explain," said Elvis, taking his arm and leading him to the camp bed, now straightened out and with extra blankets heaped nearby, ready to cover him.

Without attempting to explain anything, Elvis talked about the old days and what good times they'd had – even bringing a smile to Denny's face. Soon, his eyes began to glaze over, and he was easily persuaded to lie down more comfortably.

When his eyes stayed closed and his breathing was even, Elvis pulled the bedding over him and left the darkened cellar feeling virtuous having, thoughtfully, left water and a pack of sandwiches within his captive's reach.

On his drive home, a worrying thought nagged him... Had the blow from the rock damaged Denny's brain? Perhaps he could afford to turn him loose. Tomorrow he would have to do something; he couldn't keep him locked up forever – it was decision time again.

39. Meanwhile

Sarah was still exhausted, even after a night's sleep. Yesterday had been eventful – even exciting, but long.

Polly, as usual, was up and ready to serve breakfast for them both when Sarah arrived downstairs. "After we've eaten, perhaps we should bring our notes up to date," she said hopefully. "Terry has already left to check into the Station and see if any of his queries have been answered. He has left his mobile number for you to ring him, as we didn't know how long you would sleep."

Sarah said she would ring him later, giving him time to get to know his colleagues and settle in. While Polly and Pat decided what chores were of prime importance to be tackled today, she enjoyed a long call to Clarrie.

Emma was waddling about now, rather than crawling, being followed faithfully by Daxy, both loving every moment. Her latest game was pushing her bare feet near him to be licked, then giggling and squealing when it tickled. Daxy was a quick learner and lost no opportunity to make her laugh.

On a more serious note, Elly had visited Clarrie several times, especially when she was on the computer. "I know when she arrives, because I get a sudden urge to look at Map Quest," she laughed. Promising that she and Polly would visit them again as soon as possible,

Sarah replaced the receiver just as Polly walked in.

Pushing a trolley with coffee and biscuits on it, Polly forestalled protests about just having had breakfast by saying, "Coffee now, biscuits later when we've finished bringing our notes up to date." To emphasise her point she waved her notebook aloft and sat down, pen in hand. "We might start by noting all that we suspect..." she suggested, "then we can see if the whole picture fits together."

"Or where it falls apart," Sarah replied wryly. "But I agree, it will help us to focus. Starting at the end, when Denny Davies drove Perry home, all the house lights were on. They went in, and by staying with Mary until she was taken to hospital, sending Perry upstairs to check on the children, he prevented Perry from finishing off what he'd started before he left – killing his wife."

"What were the children doing while their mother was being attacked?" Polly wondered, then answered her own question... "They must have been drugged or already disposed of. In which case, it follows that they must all have been drugged."

"So now we have to find out when they were seen last, by anybody. We need to do a lot of telephoning!"

Not wasting any time, Sarah was soon talking to Barbie Ball with Bill joining in on their extension, discussing each question asked, before answering.

The week following her birthday, which must have been the second week in March, the weather was terrible, and a little boy was drowned. They had seen very little of anybody and were worried because Arthur had been interviewed by the police about the boy's cap.

Sarah put the phone on *speaker* mode so they both heard Bill say, "A few days after little Ronnie Biggs was drowned in the river, the police found his cap at the end of our lane."

"Because of the nasty rumours about poor Arthur, they searched the house and garden for any trace of the boy," said Barbie, "Finally, they admitted it could have been blown along the road from the river, where he must have fallen in. It was terrible. Arthur was never the same again - I'm sure that's what made him sell up." She was referring to an old diary, so was sure that everything was normal for the following week ...Mary with the children on the school run in her little Mini every day and Perry driving home at about six-thirty.

The weather was so much better at the weekend that she was pleased to see Perry playing with the children in the back garden... He was helping them to make a tent.

There was nothing further to learn, but Polly was sure they were on the right track. Sarah was inclined to agree. They both thought it likely that, while Perry kept the children occupied, his wife was already drugged into a sleep from which he planned she would not awake.

"If he drugged and killed the children on Friday night He could have buried them in the well then smashed it up and filled the hole with the debris and covered it over with grass cut from the font garden," Polly stated. "He had Saturday morning - after a night's sleep, to tidy it up. He would most likely have left killing his wife until it was close to the time Denny was collecting him. He would not want the blood to congeal for more than a couple of hours."

"Goodness me," Sarah's eyes widened, "Miss Marple personified – you amaze me, Polly!"

Undaunted, Polly continued... "Remember – the dog was tied up, probably barking and howling from hunger all day. I can't believe he would have thought of feeding it." Sarah was inclined to agree about the dog and had to face the fact that Polly was most likely to be right about the timing of the gruesome crimes.

Something was missing, she felt... Something said earlier had reminded her of the dreamlike moment recently when she had felt herself to be behind the driving wheel of a car, trying to steer it ...trying to see through the avalanche of rain – useless wipers swishing before her eyes...

40. Home sweet Home

It was later than he'd intended when he left Shirley's.
He put his foot down on the accelerator, hoping Denny
would still be too dozy to worry about why he was locked
in.

Earlier, to avoid having to shop, he had grabbed a
few things from the fridge. He could go to a supermarket
on his way back, to replace what he had taken, and Ellen
wouldn't be making lunch, she was going out soon, so it
was unlikely she would notice. As he walked from the
kitchen to the front door, he had heard voices in the
sitting room and was curious about who could be
visiting; it was far too early for coffee. It became clear
that the woman was a neighbour borrowing a carton of
milk...

Fridge!

He dashed back to the kitchen and grabbed a fresh
pint from the fridge door, returning quietly to the hall.
Just as he was about to enter the sitting room, the
conversation gripped him, and he stood quietly, listening.
The haunted house was only two doors away from her
and the neighbour, Greta, was nervous because her
husband had volunteered her to babysit there. It seemed
a neighbourly thing to do because she knew the children
well, but her husband, when he saw how worried she

was, said he couldn't go with her because he had a darts match to play.

It was too good a chance for Elvis to ignore, so he entered and joined the company.

Offering the milk to the woman, he told Ellen that he was off to check the house again and do a bit in the garden – then said he'd heard about the ghost and would happily sit with the woman on Saturday if she would like company – and didn't mind watching football!

Before the visitor could reply, Ellen laughed, "Greta, that's an excellent idea. We won't have to watch Elvie's football and you'll not have to worry about the haunting!"

"I've probably met your husband if he's in the *Grocer's* team," Elvis smiled, and we already have my wife's approval. Greta smiled a little uncertainly but, as long as it freed him to go to the pub with a clear conscience, she was sure Carlos would gladly agree.

Elvis sang along with the car radio as he covered the miles through villages and hamlets in record time, hoping that whatever awaited him at home would not spoil his mood. The quietness as he let himself into the cellar was alarming; he had prepared himself for a verbal attack from an outraged Denny.

In fact, the man appeared to be fast asleep.

It was imperative that he should find out what had been discussed with those two women and he wondered if Denny knew anything about the strange man they were with... Could he be a mate of Theo Penn perhaps?

In any case, he must wake sleeping beauty and feed

him, so that they could enjoy another long heart-to-heart. Depending on what he found out he had to decide on his next step ...putting his guest to sleep for another twenty-four hours or putting him in his final resting place.

"Phew... I don't know what's the matter with me these days," whispered Denny as he responded to another shake of his shoulder. "I can't stay awake. Thanks for bringing me food again."

It was a relief, in a way, that Denny's mood was placid, even friendly, but how much did he remember from earlier times and any recent discussions with his new friends? He had to risk reminding him or he would learn nothing of value.

Three hours later, it seemed to him that Denny's memory of the night they had returned to find Mary beaten, and the kids gone, no longer existed. He was more anxious to hear about the thugs who were after him, and to know why? The elaborate reason for threatened harm tested Perry's story-telling skills, but it seemed to satisfy the 'victim', who happily linked it to his friendship with Scoop.

"He comes across all sorts of unsavoury characters in his search for news." He frowned and then added, "It could well be because I told him about a gang of youngsters brawling outside the cinema a few weeks ago."

"It could indeed be that, but when I found you there was no sign of them," Perry encouraged. "Can you remember how many days you were wandering, lost, before I rescued you? It must have been at least three.

Then I brought you here because you wouldn't let me take you to the hospital or the police, would you?"

"No, that's right, they really scared me. They must have followed me from *The Grocer's*, where we met. It was great to see you after all those years. Then they must have bashed my head in – it still hurts."

"So, would you like to rest here again, or go home? I could go and check your place now and take you back tomorrow, if you'd feel safer..."

Elvis had already fed him another powder and was beginning to think it would be less risky to take him to the hospital and report how he had 'found' him. After all, what could Denny possibly have remembered about that night that had not cropped up at the time? The woman was interested in the ghost, not in him...

Thinking of the ghost reminded him about his Saturday night 'date'. Although he didn't expect to see Mary's ghost there, he was eager to see the place she was supposedly haunting. He didn't want to be seen in the pub again, so it was better than a night in with his wife and Shirley. In fact, it would perhaps be better if he dropped out of sight altogether, in that part of the world.

It was time he and Ellen came home.

41. Stray Thoughts

Sarah still couldn't shake the feeling that Denny Davies was alive somewhere, even if not well. It was a strange sensation and worrying.

DI Whitelow had now, officially, been introduced to Spook and heard his first-hand version of the abduction and murder. With the additional information they had learned about the old water-well disappearing, virtually overnight, and the possibility of the lights being on before Perry left the house, Terry did not doubt that there was a strong chance that Perry was behind the attack on his wife and it was possible that he was a multi-murderer. All he needed now was proof.

Sarah's worries were interrupted by a telephone call from Clarrie. She was ecstatic about her new website and said she had already sent the address to her, by email. "Stevie has done a fantastic job and wouldn't take a penny! He says he hasn't started his business yet. When he does, I promised to recommend him. In the meantime, I invited him to our dinner party tonight, but he can't make it – he has another engagement. Rowena is staying overnight afterwards, by the way, so the following day we are going ghost-hunting... Must dash – lots to do – love to Polly – stay out of trouble, you two."

Still laughing, although slightly perturbed about the ghost-hunting, Sarah repeated the instruction to Polly, who said, "Cheeky madam!" with a smile on her face. While the house phone was engaged with Clarrie and

Sarah's chat, she'd had a call on her mobile from Gavin, who wondered if he and Dave could come for an update on all that had happened. "I said they could come for tea at four-o-clock, unless you wish to change it, in which case I'll ring him straight back now."

"No need to ring back, that's fine," agreed Sarah, "I suppose that means you will be baking goodies this morning. I'll let Terry know. He hasn't met them yet, so might like to come home before they leave, if not for their arrival."

After leaving a message for Terry at the Police station, she settled down to collect her thoughts and mull over the prolonged absence of Denny; did she feel that he was alive, because she didn't want to face the alternative? There was no answer to that, so she turned to the folder Polly had left with her; a folder full of notes, all printed neatly on A4 paper. Sarah penned a note of her own on the top sheet... *Order more paper!*

Every time she tried to imagine what Perry had done on that long-ago Saturday – the day the children had disappeared, and his wife was attacked – she was distracted again by finding herself behind the wheel, driving a car, with rain obscuring the road ahead.

It was terrifying.

What did it mean?

This time, instead of flinching and backing away from the vision, knowing it was just a dream in her head, she gripped the "wheel" steadily and held her breath.

More aware now of her surroundings, she saw a toy dangling below the rear-view mirror. She just had time to register that it was a cute monkey waving a tankard in one hand and a bottle in the other, when a huge gust of wind seemed to heave the car into the centre of the road and something heavy landed on top of the bonnet.

Staring at her, his face crushed against the streaming wet glass was a small boy. His cap was wedged behind a wiper.

The shock restored Sarah to the present, where she was sitting comfortably, warm and dry. One thing was clear, there might well be another death attributable to Perry. If this was the missing boy thought to have been swept into the river and drowned, it would have been only a week or two before his three step-children also disappeared. Could he have taken the boy's body from the scene of the road accident and used the well in his own garden for the first time, establishing its effectiveness for disposing of bodies?

According to Polly's notes, Arthur noticed heaped soil in the front garden after one of the dogs died. A few days later the same spot was flattened, almost hollow. Having thrown the boy's body in the well, covering it with the remains of the dog would have misled any torches directed down the well in a search and confused signals from even the most up-to-date ground-penetrating radar that might have been used in those days.

In the event, no such search was made by the police, and his success may well have been what inspired him to rid himself of both his wife and the children. By breaking up the walls of the well and, behind the screen provided by the tent, using the stones and then loose soil, to fill it to the surface, it was unlikely to attract attention. Lifting grass from the front garden, to cover the damaged area, would not have taken more than an hour or two... Very clever.

Sarah's mind wandered back to Denny. What had he needed to tell her that was so important?

Were Geoff Bryce and Mary together now – in which case, was she still haunting the estate house? If her children were in spirit, why had they not already been with their father, Geoff?

The answer came to her immediately and she knew that he was so consumed with anger, that Geoff was going nowhere until Perry was punished for his actions and, having found him, Mary was going nowhere without Geoff. She sighed, hoping it wouldn't be long before justice was served and life for everyone, either on earth or in heaven was on an even keel.

Polly served a light lunch and considered all that Sarah had surmised from the notes.

It put into words what they had all been thinking and she wondered if Scoop had any more news about Denny. "Should we now conclude that Perry is responsible for Denny's absence from home?" she asked Sarah.

Sarah couldn't say but did suggest that they should ask what Gavin thought. He'd seen them together on the night Denny disappeared. "I wonder if he heard their conversation, or could tell whether it was friendly, or not."

"Let us suppose that Perry did take Denny away from his home, where would he hold him?" Polly was puzzled but Sarah reminded her that Terry was checking Perry's home address – after all, he and his wife were only visiting her sister whose house was on the same road as Pete and Peggy's.

Realising the time, Polly went off to clear the dining room and prepare for tea. When the kitchen was straight again she went upstairs to tidy herself. Despite all the worrisome things happening around her she was happy and so lucky to be with Sarah. It was no hardship to take care of her and exciting to be involved in all the problems that came her way.

42. Second Thoughts

Their visitors arrived on time and were eager to start exchanging information. At last, when Polly was happy that everyone had their food and drink of choice, she sat down to talk. Sarah and Polly didn't want to confide their deepest suspicions about Elvis, but they needed to know as much as they could about him since his reappearance in the area.

Eventually, Gavin mentioned seeing him with Denny, on the night before Denny disappeared. "He was alone in the bar for over an hour, I think, before Denny Davies recognised him and went to sit with him. In the old days they used to come in together at the weekends but weren't in my age group, so I can't say I knew either of them."

Polly had been housekeeper for Stephen Grey's parents for years before he married Sarah. Stephen and Sarah had moved away before Polly had married with a home of her own, but she had held her position with the elder Grey family and had never lost touch with Sarah.

While it was amazing that she and her own children had all settled finally in the same county, it would have been even more amazing if she had failed to keep track of all their friends. Thinking about this, she asked if Gavin had known Mary and indeed anyone from this area. He'd never seen Mary but was sure he had met Theo Penn when he was a night-watchman at the hospice. Gavin's father was a patient there for several months before he died.

Gavin and Dave were keener to discuss Pete's problem. Everything had been unchanged as far as the haunting was concerned, until the last week or two, which was why Pete had suggested that they needed to tell Sarah.

Holly, who was only four years old didn't take much notice when she was called Babs, and Andy who was seven and Amy, five, had grown accustomed to the Kitchen lady calling them Toby and Annie. It didn't bother them. They told their parents, who had never made a big deal of their being able to see someone who was invisible to everyone else. Lots of children had invisible friends, although they were usually other children, not grownups.

"It was something best ignored, they thought," Dave came to their defence, "and the ghost seemed to care for them. But lately, things have changed," he sighed. "The children say the woman stares at them, muttering about their clothes and hair. She asked them a few days ago if they had seen Elly; they know nothing at all about anyone called Elly and it's now beginning to worry them."

It was obvious that Dave was upset and although Sarah told him that Elly was a little girl and was no threat, it was clear that Mary needed to be guided to leave their house. She knew Geoff Bryce would help, when he was ready, himself – he would want her to go with him, to the place where she would be reunited with her own three children, if their suspicions were correct, but from what Dave said, Mary was not going to move on, yet, and she knew that Geoff was not ready to try and persuade her. She said, with honesty that she could deal with the problem. He need not fret about it any longer.

They were relieved to hear that Sarah could deal with Mary, but the thing they both were most keen to talk about was that Pete and Peggy had needed a babysitter for Saturday night. "We are in the darts team and have a match we can't miss, and they were reluctant to ask you again because you are sitting on Monday," Gavin said. He waved down the protestations that it would have been no trouble. "No, no, Peggy would have stayed home herself, but wants to support Pete and the team. Then – guess what! A neighbour, another team player, volunteered his wife, Greta. She was upset and nervous about the house being haunted and told a friend whose husband volunteered straight away to babysit with her and his wife agreed that he should." Gavin laughed... "Have you ever heard anything like it?"

"Don't worry, said Dave," seeing the expressions on their faces, "We have checked them out and they are both respectable, responsible adults!"

"Who are they then? We may know them." Polly asked.

Gavin shook his head – unable to remember Greta's surname... "But the guy is Elvis Perry – apparently he used to live around here."

They stared at Gavin in astonishment, but before

they could react the front doorbell rang.

"That will be DI Whitelow, Sarah said as Polly went to answer.

Standing up immediately, the two men said it was time they left so they'd go while the door was open and leave them in peace. Sarah didn't protest – she was too shaken to say anything other than it had been nice to see them.

Terry was worried when he heard about Perry's proposed sitting at the Fletchers, as they all were. Why would Perry want to visit their house? It could only be curiosity. Perhaps he'd heard that the ghost was thought to be his deceased wife? They speculated on what might happen have happened if Gavin hadn't mentioned it in passing – not knowing that Perry was '*a person of interest*', under investigation.

There was no way they could sanction his being anywhere near the children, but Terry couldn't risk Perry discovering that he was under suspicion of anything.

"Perhaps we could move the children out of harm's way," Polly suggested. "The woman sounds too timid to go upstairs as long as quiet reigns, and the dog might well have gone with the children, so Elvis Perry wouldn't even be threatened by it."

"Thanks Polly," Terry said, after looking thoughtfully at Sarah, as if for inspiration, "you have given me an idea. I need an introduction to the Fletcher family as soon as possible."

"I'll ring Peggy now," Polly volunteered, "We could probably go straight away."

"Perfect, we need to act fast." Terry looked at his watch and stood up, ready to leave, as Polly replaced the phone with a smile. To her surprise, he suggested she took her own car as he needed to spend a few hours discussing his idea with the parents.

After they departed Sarah put her feet up and switched on the TV news, but she couldn't concentrate. Would Mary leave the house with the children? She thought not, but did it matter, either way? Why did Perry want to be inside the house anyway? Unless someone had said anything inadvertently to arouse his suspicions...

If they were right about Perry's being guilty of beating Mary – and murdering her children – and she was haunting the house, would seeing him revive all her memories? If it did, what could she do ...show herself?

The drone of the television and her churning thoughts gradually lulled her to sleep.

When Polly returned she was pleased to see Sarah getting some rest ...she would have time to make something really special for dinner.

43. A Risk Too Far?

After another night of normal, unaided sleep, Denny was rational and eager to discuss the ruffians who had assaulted him. Elvis had risked withholding the sleeping powder to discover if Denny's memories of their evening in the *Grocer's* and what followed – had really been lost.

He tested Denny with several questions and found that he accepted completely the existence of the young villains who had attacked him and totally believed he'd been rescued by Elvis. "Honestly, I'm ready to face going home now. It was very kind of you to look after me, but I need to get back there. We can't let the hoodlums win, can we?"

Perry resisted his pleas for another hour or two. He continued to question Denny about his two new friends but as far as Denny knew they were writing a history of village life and ghosts and stuff – and he'd never believed in ghosts, so he couldn't help them. He liked going there to eat because one of them was a fantastic cook and baked almost every day. "You should try her sausage rolls and apple pie," he said dreamily.

Two hours later, Perry left the police station with a smile on his face. At Denny's insistence they had gone first to check his house, but, of course had no keys. It was quite a circus after that. Scoop had to be called, as he had one to the back door. He in turn called the police, who turned up at Denny's, just after Scoop arrived and they had let themselves in.

Denny flatly refused to be taken to the station like a criminal and Elvis overheard him giving the story of his 'ordeal' to the officer in charge. Perfect, he would never have believed that Denny was so susceptible to suggestion. He was describing some of the thugs and, in minute detail, what they were wearing; notebooks were out taking it all down.

Eventually Denny agreed to being taken to the hospital to be checked, and they insisted that he should stay in overnight. He stopped making a fuss when Elvis promised to collect him at lunchtime to take him home. Elvis thought he might well spend the afternoon with him, but it was Saturday and there was no way he was missing his evening 'date' with Greta.

He had been reading up on ghosts and it was accepted that, if they wished, they could appear to anybody; you didn't have to be psychic. Fear itself often creates an atmosphere that attracts ghosts ...and so on!

It was rubbish, of course.

In any case he wasn't frightened of any ghost; they couldn't take advantage of him on that score. He really wasn't quite sure what he would gain by looking inside the so-called haunted house, but it would give him a chance to get close to the site of the old well, just to check it was still "well" hidden. Smiling at his own joke, he did consider that although he wouldn't see Mary, if she did happen to be there, she might well see him...

Was she still out of her mind? Would she remember

what he'd done? Too bad, if she did! She couldn't tell anybody could she...!

Perry had been surprisingly reluctant to leave him, but each time Denny repeated his story to anyone who would listen, it sounded more convincing. In his latest account, one of the gang smoked non-stop and had a squint in one eye.

It was disconcerting, but his rash removal of Denny could have resulted in a much worse scenario for him. It was a relief to have got through the ordeal unscathed. Whatever Denny had discussed with his nosey friends surely couldn't matter after all these years. Life could be worse he reflected as he drove back to the estate.

News of Denny's return had spread fast. Terry rang Sarah immediately and, within minutes, she had received calls from other friends asking if it could be true. Someone had seen him at the hospital and said Elvis Perry seemed glued to his side – apparently having rescued him.

44. Adding Two and Two

As soon as he was allowed visitors, Sarah and Polly went to see Denny in hospital. It was Friday afternoon and they missed Perry by only half an hour. He had lingered out of sight for several minutes, listening to Denny describe to the nurse how frightening his ordeal had been and how grateful he was to his brave friend, Elvis. Perry was, consequently, satisfied that the blow to Denny's head had magically removed all memory of what really happened.

Denny was delighted to see them, and the nurse smiled as she moved an extra chair to his bedside and warned them not to tire her patient or let him get overexcited. As she left the room he was still talking about the terrible night he was abducted... "I thought they were going to kill me..."

Sarah was dismayed and whispered to Polly, "It doesn't seem possible that Perry performed an act of mercy. Something else is going on, I'm sure." To their surprise, Denny's expression changed, and he indicated that he was listening to the sound of the nurse's footsteps retreating.

His faraway air disappeared, and he said, in a normal tone of voice, "Thank God you've come straight away. I was afraid the doctor would have put off visitors and I really can't keep this up much longer." After coming around from the knockout blow to the back of his head he was terrified. "I was doubled up on the back seat of a car, not knowing where he was taking me, or why, but I couldn't believe he intended letting me go again, after attacking me like that."

"I assume you mean that Perry was the one who attacked you?" Sarah said, and Denny nodded.

Until he knew why he was being taken away, he decided to 'play dumb' – asking where they were and what happened seemed the best ploy.

Polly applauded and praised him for being so brave "It's a Godsend that you came around enough to assess what was happening, before demanding to know why he attacked you!"

While he was still faking drowsiness Perry tried to question him about why *'those two busybodies'* he'd met were reaping up the murder of his wife, Mary. As soon as he realised what Perry was demanding of him, it was wiser to pretend complete ignorance and confine himself to questioning where he was and how he'd come to be there.

When Perry started making up the scenario he wanted Denny to remember, Denny obliged, lulling his captor into a false sense of security. "I knew," he told them, "that he would kill me, as he had his family."

"How did you ever come to be sure that he did?" Polly asked, "we had only touched on the possibility when we spoke last."

"Yes, dear lady, and that was why I left the message about coming to see you both the next morning.

Unfortunately, Perry was sure that we three had been discussing his actions on the fateful weekend. He wanted to know what questions you had asked and what else I'd said, but I kept playing dumb and just asked about the youngsters who attacked me. I told him I thought I'd seen one of them before."

It was evident that he had managed to convince Perry how thankful he was to have been rescued from them. "Well, we have a lot to tell you," said Sarah, "...and thank heaven you are really well and not out of your mind – you had us all worried. We must keep up the pretext to everyone else for the time being – and please tell us why you were coming to see me. What had you discovered?"

"It was just before we left *The Grocers*. He took something from his pocket and a slip of paper fell on the floor. While he was getting our drinks at the bar I picked it up and saw it was a receipt... The thing is, it reminded me of a receipt from the chemist that I'd found in my car where he had sat, on the day after the murders.

It hadn't meant anything to me then, but it was for four packets of something with a funny name. This time it was for one pack, but the name of the drug suddenly meant something to me. It was prescribed for me a few months ago." After a dramatic pause he told them. "They were sleeping powders."

"Perhaps he doesn't sleep well," said Polly, "we mustn't leap to conclusions."

"I think in this case," Sarah said, "we need only consider that he apparently had a large quantity of sleeping powders on hand. If I remember from when

Clarrie was injured, there would have been ten doses in a box and, if he did as we suspect, he would have needed a large quantity in readiness to keep his whole family comatose for at least two days..." She sighed. "What a cruel man. How can we prove it after so many years?"

Denny suddenly put on a foolish grin as the door opened. The nurse was about to tell them their time was up, but Denny gave her a happy smile, pleading for another five minutes. "Well, just three then," she said, and went off shaking her head indulgently.

"It was just as well that I made the connection," Denny said quickly, "because, to keep a clear head, I had to avoid drinking anything I hadn't poured myself. I managed, under a blanket, to pour the stuff he gave me into the plastic bag my sandwiches had been in, or down the back of the settee I was on. He now thinks the bash he gave me on my head has damaged my brain and we mustn't let him know any different. Please be careful not to let word get out – you know what people are like."

Exactly three minutes later the nurse re-entered tapping her watch and was pleased to see that his two visitors were ready to leave.

45. One Step Nearer

After leaving Denny they rang Terry and he decided to meet them back at Sarah's, "...at teatime," he added hopefully. Polly heard him and said he was in luck, she had baked before they left home that morning. It was a clever idea to talk where there was no risk of being overheard. What they had to tell him, bringing him up to date, especially about Denny's current predicament was too sensitive to leak out.

"We have a couple of hours to spare, so there's something I'd like to do before we go home," Sarah announced, and followed up with a request for a pen and paper. Polly immediately tore a blank page from her notebook and handed it over with her ball-point pen. Although curious, she held her questions back and waited. The drawing Sarah produced looked like a man with a pillbox hat dancing wildly, waving a bottle and a mug.

When Sarah stopped to show her and asked what it looked like, she laughed at Polly's reply. "I never was good at drawing ...so what can I do to make it look like a monkey?" Polly suggested putting four hands on it and giving it a tail. Big ears helped. When they were both happy with it, Sarah described her recurring vision of herself driving a car (at which Polly raised one eyebrow but refrained from comment). Ignoring her, Sarah continued to describe the horrendous storm and not being able to see beyond the cascading water and swishing, useless windscreen washers.

Polly nodded, understanding.

In the last vision, Sarah explained that she had seen a mascot hanging from the mirror in front of her. "If I show this to someone who knew Elvis Perry and his car in those days – I hope they will recognise it. So, who do you think we should ask?"

Polly had no doubt who they should try first. She said that Bill and Barbie often saw Perry driving up and down to the cottages and he had even stopped to apologise to them about the noisy dogs a couple of weeks before the fatal attack on Perry's wife.

Putting the car in gear immediately, without waiting for agreement, she started driving to the Balls' house where they had recently enjoyed supper. Sarah rarely used her mobile but thought it only polite to warn them that she and Polly were on their way and needed to ask them one question that wouldn't interrupt them for long.

It was difficult to convince Barbie that they really couldn't stay, even for a few minutes, as they were themselves expecting someone to call on them at home within the hour. Finally, Barbie accepted that they were in a hurry and while she was asking when they could come for a meal, Bill arrived in the hallway and they had to explain again. He had been staring at the drawing in Sarah's hand and said, "Goodness me, I haven't seen one like that for a long while – it's a car mascot isn't it?"

"Can you recall where you saw it?" Sarah asked,

"That's why we've called." Without hesitation he said that he had seen one like it in Elvis Perry's car – actually, the only one he had ever seen.

He couldn't understand why people had such things dangling in front of them when they should have their eyes on the road – downright dangerous. Sarah was delighted and asked if he could email her, confirming where, and when, he had seen it, fixing the date as accurately as he could. Bill said he would be pleased to help and rightly supposed that he should not mention it to Perry, if they met.

As they drove away, Polly remarked that they hadn't met anyone so far who liked Perry. She supposed both his wives must have, but in Mary's position, recently widowed, it was likely that she would have welcomed his help with the children and been heavily influenced by his apparent kindness. He would undoubtedly have put on an act to convince her of his sincerity.

Terry arrived within twenty minutes of their reaching home and they soon settled down to enjoy tea while exchanging news.

Terry now had Perry's address and Sarah confirmed that Denny had been held in a cellar, which might well have been there. The police who interviewed Denny, when he was brought back by his "rescuer", Elvis Perry, had reported to Terry that he was not injured badly and would be able to identify the gang members when they were caught. They were very happy with the outcome.

Terry had been sceptical and was delighted to hear the real version of what had happened and to know that

Denny was indeed well. They would certainly keep that knowledge to themselves and there was no point in interviewing him yet anyway.

Sarah showed him her drawing of the car mascot and related her vision of the storm and the boy crashing into the windscreen. With Bill's email confirmation that he had seen it in Perry's car at the time of the little boy's disappearance, it was something else to hold against Perry. Although it was enough to convince the three of them, it was not evidence that could be used to convict him.

Terry was pleased and said, "So, now we're thinking that just after he killed the dog and buried it at the front of the cottages, he had an accident in the storm – killed the boy and removed him from the scene. He threw the body in the well and lifted the dog's carcass from the front garden, throwing it on top of the boy, along with soil from the dog's grave."

"That fits in with what Arthur – or was it Barbie? – said at the time – that the ground, which had been a mound one day was hollowed the day after." Polly was ecstatic. "And perhaps that's what gave him the idea of putting the children in the well too. He might have been wishing to get out of his marriage for a long time."

Terry agreed that evidence appeared to be mounting fast against Elvis Perry, but he had already mooted the idea with Sarah's friend Alec Holme, his Chief Super, that they might need to dig up the well. That was still an option, but he would like something concrete to back it up.

After making a couple of telephone calls, Terry told

them not to worry, he would deal with it. Theo had offered him his spare room, as it would be much nearer to the Police HQ and the chief had arranged for the station to rent it officially. He said it would be useful to have it available, even after Terry left. He had also allowed Terry to book out one of the unmarked cars, so he now had transport.

They were sorry that he was leaving them, but Terry promised to bring them up to date and would probably call in every day. They must not worry; things were going well.

46. Alone at last

As promised, Elvis had picked Denny up from the hospital on Saturday afternoon and taken him home. Denny kept up the pretence of being apprehensive: making sure the place was safe and that nobody was in hiding, ready to attack him as soon as he was alone. Elvis assured him that everything was secure and the police most likely were keeping an eye on him anyway. They wouldn't let him come to harm.

Elvis was glad to get away and Denny, in truth, wanted to be left on his own. It went against the grain to have to appear stupid.

He wished Sarah and Polly would call on him frequently until this charade was over. If not, he'd have to emigrate... He couldn't live like this forever.

He thought over what Elvis had said about babysitting for someone tonight. It sounded most unlikely, but he'd said that it was a favour for some chap who had volunteered his wife. She couldn't get out of it, and he wasn't able to sit with her – darts night of course, so Elvis volunteered to go with her for company.

It didn't sound credible to him. There must be something in it for Elvis and he could rule the woman out, no matter how attractive she was!

Bored and lonely, he rang Sarah. Perhaps she and

Polly could come over for a drink – then maybe he could take them somewhere for a meal... There was no answer. Had she mentioned that they would be out tonight when he saw her... Had that been today? No. it was Saturday today – it was yesterday when they'd met at the hospital.

He owed Scoop a drink and he would certainly be fascinated to hear what had really happened over the last few days. So far, Scoop had only heard Perry's version making him out to be a hero. He had no idea that Perry was a villain so yes, Scoop should be told. No longer a reporter, he was a feature writer, and Denny could trust him to keep his mouth shut until he could write up the story himself.

He was lucky to find Scoop in.

At first, the poor man was at a loss, whether to accept or refuse Denny's invitation to visit him for a drink. He'd had other plans for tonight and Denny was hardly good company now. He hadn't even recognised him at the hospital, as he babbled non-stop about what a hero Perry had been.

Denny interrupted his thoughts. "We could go out to eat somewhere, if you like: my treat." Sensing Scoop's hesitation, he added that he had quite a story to tell him. "Not for publication at this point, but interesting enough to make you glad you came."

Three hours later, as Scoop returned home after an excellent meal with a completely normal Denny, he marvelled at the man's shrewdness. The way he had, and was still, outwitting the man who certainly would not have hesitated to kill him, was amazing. Being also in the confidence of DI Whitelow, he was happy to help

Denny in any way he could to conceal the real facts. If that meant spending more time with him to safeguard his sanity, then so be it. What were friends for?

47. The Babysitters

On Saturday evening, Pete and Peggy were pleased when Greta arrived five minutes early. "The children are probably asleep by now and they usually sleep soundly so," Peggy said, "unless they call out or cry, you should have no need to go up. I'd really rather they didn't see you, especially Holly as you are a stranger to her."

Greta gave a sigh of relief. "I was really nervous about being here alone, because I've heard you have a ghost, so I hope you don't mind but a friend's husband, Elvie Perry, is coming to sit with me."

Peggy said that of course she didn't mind, she had met Mrs Perry, and nodded when Greta added, "His sister-in-law lives along the road." Her eyes widened as she glanced around her. "But hasn't he arrived yet? I hope you won't leave until he comes."

To their relief, the doorbell rang – they had counted on being on their way by seven-thirty.

"He is very welcome if it makes you more comfortable," said Pete, hoping it wouldn't cost him double!"

Peggy took Greta to the kitchen to show her where to find a snack and a drink. "There might not be enough for two, but please feel free to put together anything else you can find to feed Mr Perry."

When they reached the car, Pete looked back at the house and frowned. "I hope all goes well tonight – but I'm glad you agreed to come with me." He relaxed and smiled. "Team Fletcher needs all the support it can get!" Then he rang to let the *Grocer's* team know they were on their way.

Elvis looked around as the parents left, and noted that the chairs looked comfortable, the room was warm, and the television was enormous. With a sigh of relief, he took the armchair where the remote control was within reach, and asked Greta, "Did they show you where the bar is?" When she looked at him blankly, he said, "Drinks. Beer or whisky... Maybe there's something in the fridge?" Greta was unhappy but remembering that she had seen a few bottles and fruit juice, she went back to the kitchen.

By the time she returned, the TV was going full blast and with a surge of annoyance she asked him to please turn down the volume, or they wouldn't hear the children if they woke up. She couldn't be sure that they had slept through and were still asleep, after all the noise, but hoped they were. He did as she asked, with a grunt that might have been an apology.

TV didn't interest her unless it was the news or an interesting film, so she picked up one of the magazines, which Peggy had left on the coffee table for her to read.

It wasn't easy to concentrate on even the most interesting article because he was a noisy viewer – constantly sighing or shouting at the screen, as if the people on it could hear him. About an hour later she thought she heard movement upstairs and asked him to turn the sound down.

After doing so, he went to the open door to listen. She first thought *how kind of him,* then changed her mind when he walked to the kitchen saying he needed a top-up anyway.

He returned bearing a couple more bottles but did have the grace to lower the volume slightly, for which she thanked him. She decided that in another hour, if the match he was watching had finished, she would suggest that they ate the food Peggy had prepared.

Things weren't so bad really, she thought, she was comfortable, with reading matter she enjoyed, and Elvie Perry could have turned out to be much worse. At least he wasn't bombarding her with small-talk!

An announcement on the TV made her look up... It should end in about five minutes, so Greta made her way to the kitchen. In the hall, she stopped and listened for a moment; satisfied that all was quiet upstairs, she went to compile a meal for them both.

An outburst of cheering marked the end of the match as she re-entered the room and settled down again. Perry was joining in, clapping his hands. *Thank goodness* Greta thought, he's still in a good mood...

It was as the noise died down that she heard something strange.

It didn't sound like a child...

Incredibly, it sounded like the low growl of a dog!

Elvis turned the sound off, as she immediately asked, and they both listened. He was out into the hallway in a flash, not really believing what he could hear. He had grabbed a poker on the way out of his chair, ready to deal with anything.

What he didn't expect to see was Butcher crouching at the top of the stairs... *Butcher, the dog he had hated and beaten to death years ago.*

As Perry backed away in astonishment and horror – scarcely believing his eyes – the dog lifted its head and crawled across the landing towards him, teeth bared. The menacing growl rumbled through the stillness even more fiercely. Still inside the room, Greta could only imagine what was happening and was petrified.

He'd dismissed the tales he'd heard about the ghostly dog, yet here it was! Summoning up what little courage he had, Perry told himself that the dog was not alive, it couldn't hurt him and, gripping the fire-iron, he moved slowly up the stairs to meet what must be an apparition – he'd had too much to drink, that was it – surely?

The huge dog crouched and edged nearer to him, lips curled. The growls grew louder, and it was about to spring when another vision appeared to him.

In the open doorway of the children's bedroom was a figure draped in white. From the landing there was no light on the woman, but the moonlight shining into the room beyond created a halo around her slim body, and when she spoke he almost fainted... Sadly, quietly, she whispered, *"Oh, Elvis... Why? Why... How could you be so cruel?"*

As she stepped closer, her arms wide, the dog uttered a howl of anger, crouched, and leapt at him.

For Perry, it was too much, and in trying to escape the frenzied hound he tumbled backwards down the stairs.

Greta, numb with fear, heard the snarls and whispers and then a shriek from Perry as he crashed down the stairs ...knocking the hall table flying, scattering the telephone, ornaments and flowers all over the floor.

She froze, terrified...

In the sudden eerie stillness, she forced herself to get to her feet to see what had happened.

The smashed vase, with its razor-like shards, hindered her, in her thin-soled shoes, as she tried to reach the man who was supposed to protecting her – the flowers were scattered in pools of water. He was curled, unconscious, maybe dead, against the front door...

What had happened?

What should she do?

She had to get help, ring someone – emergency – an ambulance – she decided... Then she saw the telephone receiver; it had landed under his body and the cord stretched beyond it. At its end, the instrument purred softly, at which point, she fainted.

48. The Morning After

When Clarrie rang on Sunday to tell her how big a success her dinner party had been, Sarah was forced to demonstrate a great deal of patience, to listen quietly until her daughter talked herself to a standstill.

She opened her mouth long enough to say she was pleased everything had gone well, when Clarrie launched into a list of everything on the menu and how she had to cook some special dishes she hadn't tried before to suit Adam's diet and how everyone liked what she had cooked for him so she would make the same for her and Polly when they next came...

Sarah's mouth opened again, but Clarrie hadn't finished, and again interrupted to say that Rowena and Adam had both been in Brunei and other places at the same time and he was so interesting – he's writing a book – not fiction – something really complicated about world transport. He will let us know when it's published...

Before Sarah could comment, Clarrie said something was boiling and, anyway, she would let her go now... "I hope I didn't wake you, but I had to let you know that all went well before Rowena and I go out on our ghost-hunting trip... Love to Polly – please thank her for sending the winning recipe – love you too..." Whether Sarah's *'Bye then'* carried across the line before the 'receiver clicked down, she didn't know.

She wasn't upset.

She was just contented that Clarrie was happy.

Polly came in at the end of the call and was pleased when she heard that her recipe had met with approval all round. Polly wondered if Gavin and Dave would drop in to update them, and at that moment the phone rang again. Terry, who they hadn't seen since Polly left him at the Fletchers' wanted them to know that all was well, and he would come to see them this evening.

It seemed that Perry had survived his babysitting but was currently in custody in a police cell; it wasn't clear why. Polly asked her what had happened at the Fletchers, but Sarah said she didn't know all the details and preferred to wait for Terry before speculating.

As always, when there was nothing else holding her attention, Polly happily returned to the kitchen to bake. On her way out, she commented that they hadn't heard from Theo for a while. As Terry was lodging with him Sarah said that if ill, they would have heard. However, deciding it would do no harm to make sure, Sarah telephoned Theo. She was confident that Terry would have brought him up-to-date about Denny's *recovery* and wondered if he knew about Perry's arrest.

There was no reply, which was odd, as he had no car and disliked public transport for shopping, preferring things to be delivered.

Theo would miss Terry when he returned to his normal duties, after the situation was resolved, but by that time Theo's circle of friends would be much wider.

He had been quite isolated when they first met and

hadn't mixed confidently with others. He was certainly happier now.

When Terry rang again, asking if he could bring Theo with him that evening, Sarah was delighted and invited them for dinner. Of course. Polly was too, and immediately started planning the meal.

There must have been other developments in the next hour, because Terry rang again and asked if they could cope with Denny and Scoop as well! Before she could reply he said they would bring ample supplies of wine and beer.

She seized the moment to ask if it would be an idea to invite Gavin and Dave – and perhaps Peggy and Pete Fletcher as they were the people most concerned. Terry agreed that the family should be there too, but it had seemed too large a gathering for Polly to consider coping.

Polly was not in the least dismayed – the dining room could seat ten and, as she said, their freezer was too full anyway and could do with a clear out!

They were both aware that something of importance had occurred. Whatever had happened, so far, had been kept under wraps, otherwise, the telephone would have been ringing non-stop all day asking for confirmation of rumours.

"It seems that we might be the first to hear the latest developments," said Polly, unable to conceal how much she was looking forward to what was going to be '*quite a party*', as she put it.

While Polly was fully occupied preparing the evening meal, Sarah seized the chance to go onto the computer to check her emails. There was one from Jamie, who was eager to tell her that he'd taken his mother to visit Dora.

Surprisingly, things went well.

Dora accepted that she had been responsible for putting his parents through years of agony and was extremely nervous at first, about meeting Jean Deeds, but she need not have worried. Robert and Jean had both taken the line that Dora rescued Jamie and, being ill, had genuinely believed him to be her own child.

Jean asked the questions that churned in her head – she wanted to hear about all the clever or funny things he had ever done, and Dora was as proud to repeat them as she would have been had he really been Joe, her own son. They parted on good terms, although Dora wept. Jean instinctively knew that Dora imagined that she would not be visited a second time and assured her that there was no need to fret – they would keep in touch.

The only other mail Sarah had was from Rowena's mother who said how happy she was that Rowena had a close friend like Clarrie. Rowena had enjoyed being included in her dinner party and thrilled about the planned ghost-hunting trip... She seemed to think Sarah was going with them! Sarah had no idea if more such trips were planned, but they would certainly be without her!

Having deleted all the unwanted messages, she was about to shut down when another arrived.

Recognising the name of the sender, she opened it eagerly. She had often wondered how the boy was. Bobby Goswell had been about eleven or twelve when she first met him, so must now be in his mid-teens. Sarah remembered how he had guarded from everyone his ability to see and hear ghosts. His relief and delight were apparent when Sarah assured him that he was not crazy but was wise anyway not to speak of it to all and sundry.

Bobby had been a considerable help to her when Clarry was attacked and she hoped his news was good.

Although they'd stopped writing to each other a long time ago, he hoped she wouldn't mind his getting in touch again. He wondered if she would be interested in some of the many things he had experienced since they last met.

He said he was devastated when his father's occupation changed, and they had moved too far away to see his old friends. "However," Bobby said, "so much happened that would have scared me, if you hadn't explained how I should handle things, that I decided to write down all my experiences, as short stories."

He went on to explain that his English Language teacher, who had been checking the progress of all his writing, said they were interesting and that he now had enough words for a book. If Sarah would like to read them, he could email the manuscript in a pdf file.

Sarah answered immediately that she was delighted to hear that he was well and happy and looked forward very much to reading his book.

What an excellent idea ...perhaps she should write one! Well, time was going fast. She would see if there was anything she could do for Polly and, if not, take her book into the garden to enjoy the late afternoon sunshine before going to shower and change. Surely from now on life would return to normal ...she could only hope and pray.

49. Preparing to meet the end

As the day wore on, Sarah and Polly became increasingly perturbed about whatever might be revealed tonight.

The grapevine had revelled in stories about the haunted house and their telephone had hardly stopped ringing, for the last few hours. some callers asking for information and others eager to talk about police cars at midnight, in the usually quiet road.

The report about an ambulance was the most worrying but, in a few hours, all would be revealed.

When Denny rang to ask if they had heard about Perry's arrest, Sarah sensed his disappointment when she said that DI Whitelow had rung her. She cheered him when she said that it was the clarity of his account of his ordeal that had persuaded the police that Perry was guilty of something serious and worth arresting: not least attacking him, removing him from his home and keeping him prisoner for several days. Sarah told Denny that they had visited Perry's home and found a cellar. It was as he described it, but they would be much happier if they had positive proof that he had been imprisoned in it.

Denny understood, and commented that he had seen how carefully Perry cleared away blankets and bottles – in fact anything that would cause his wife to wonder what he'd been up to. "When I realised what he was doing, I removed something to bring away. I had forgotten it until now. Do you think I should take it to show the police?"

Sarah was staggered. How could he have been clever enough to have deceived his captor about his sanity and his lack of recall, yet forget to hand over the evidence that proved he had been in Elvis Perry's home?

She swallowed her frustration and asked how he had carried away the evidence without its being seen. Denny admitted that his first attempt failed. He'd tried to walk out with a newspaper that had the delivery address on it. Perry spotted this and took it away, promising to buy him another paper when he protested that he was in the middle of reading something.

While Perry was throwing it in a bin, his back turned, Denny collapsed to sit on the settee where he had slept. There was a hole torn in the fabric and horsehair stuffing was coming out. He said, "It was easy to pull out a handful and stuff it down my trousers but to my horror, he patted me down before we walked out of the cellar. Luckily, he didn't find it. When Scoop let us into my house, so that I could collect my own keys – and check to see if the thugs had robbed me, *he laughed* – I visited the bathroom and left my trophy in a cupboard."

"You clever thing," Sarah praised him. "You must ring Terry straight away and tell him. It will make his day."

As soon as Denny put the phone down, knowing it would take him a few minutes to look up the telephone number, Sarah rang Terry herself... She had assumed that Denny knew he would be attending their dinner party tonight, but he hadn't mentioned it, so as soon as the phone was answered, she suggested that Terry should remind him. "When you hear what he has to say, I'm sure you will not want him to miss the party!"

Without enlightening him, and to avoid occupying the line for too long, she told him to expect Denny's call within minutes and hung up. He had no time to wonder what she meant because his phone was already ringing again... Not surprisingly, it was Denny.

Everyone else was expected at eight-o-clock but Terry and Theo arrived early to prepare the evening entertainment. They unloaded equipment and set up a screen for viewing in the studio upstairs, where there was room to seat everyone comfortably. Terry suggested that they should have dinner first, so that Polly would not be inconvenienced and would be able to relax and enjoy the film they wanted to show.

It was all very mysterious and intriguing. When the two men were happy with the seating, they went down to their car and came back laden with beer and wine. There must be, without doubt, something to celebrate, and Sarah was beginning to believe that her prayers for life to return to normal would be answered – or that at least the worst was over.

50. Setting the Scene

Polly had prepared salad, with ham or a variety of cheeses for anyone who couldn't enjoy her chicken curry and was confident that there would be enough curry left over to freeze. The usual variety of Sambals to accompany the curry was complete, with extra celery, cucumber, raisins and nuts, as they would complement the salad as well. The poppadums were fried and waiting in an airtight container and she would cook the rice after everyone arrived. A pre-prandial drink would take twenty minutes, so that would be no problem.

She quickly left the kitchen to prepare herself, and was back, setting the table, before the rest of the guests arrived. Sarah would have been happy to lend a hand, but Polly prided herself on her ability to cope alone and had not expected her to offer. If Sarah had offered to help, Polly would have wondered if Sarah had lost faith in her, as Sarah well knew!

While she was upstairs, she heard all the activity in their office and couldn't imagine what was happening. Having been so occupied in the kitchen, she had scarcely registered the arrival of Terry with all his paraphernalia and hurried now, to investigate.

In the office, as she passed, she saw chairs of all shapes and sizes facing a large screen... The computer had been pushed aside and a tray of glasses – also all shapes and sizes – had taken its place. The available drinks were stacked, and she noted an impressive variety. She wondered if Terry moonlighted as a barman!

Downstairs, Polly was just in time to admit the first arrivals, the Fletcher family and Gavin. Peggy was shy and a little nervous – it was her first visit to their home and she hadn't known quite what it would be like. Polly supposed that she had expected to see a crystal globe and fortune-telling tools everywhere – Tarot cards and such! Sadly, few people knew the difference between mystics and a real psychic.

After making sure everyone had drinks, Polly asked Peggy how the children had coped with all the excitement recently, but she need not have worried. Peggy said they'd spent the whole weekend with their grandparents. Dave, who had just joined them, said that it had been wonderful to have them, when they were still awake – and a real pleasure to have the whole family together, overnight.

Seeing Polly's confusion, Peggy told her, "Pete and I handed the house over to the police on Saturday morning and kept out of the way after the babysitters arrived. Greta was nervous and was obviously relieved when I told her that they were fast asleep and that she need not to go to the children unless they called her, or cried, which was extremely unlikely. Mr Perry barely spoke to me – just headed into the sitting-room to watch TV."

Polly was amazed to hear that the police had taken

over and wondered aloud what had motivated them.

Pete joined them and explained... "They'd heard of Perry's interest in the house and because of his recent behaviour, whatever that was, they needed to find out what he was up to without upsetting the children ...or us," he added, smiling. "We are not allowed to take over again until tomorrow morning. They say they intend to restore it to its former pristine order."

He nudged his wife and then gave her a hug, obviously proud of her. "After the darts match, which, by the way, we won, Peg and I went home with Dave, my father. We are worried about the family being connected somehow to a police investigation, but perhaps all this activity will scare our ghostly lady away."

Sarah, who had just welcomed the last of the guests and was standing within hearing distance, turned to tell Pete that they had lots to tell them about their ghostly guest, later, but they need have no more worries on that score. Looking doubtful rather than relieved, Pete thanked her. As if reading his mind, Sarah nodded at Polly and said, "That doesn't mean that we need to be struck off your sitters' list."

Polly laughed and commented, "Theo, especially, enjoys his night out!" She then announced that food was about to be served and the very happy crowd moved out of the sitting room to take seats at the table.

All the chatter throughout dinner was light-hearted – everyone enjoying the meal but eager for it to be over, rather than prolonged by a serious discussion of anything.

When Terry, seeing that everyone had finished

eating, suggested that they carried their remaining drink upstairs, nobody lingered, and soon they were all seated comfortably around a large screen.

Terry was in control of the film, so that he could sometimes pause it to explain anything that happened off-camera. "You must all have heard," he said, "about Perry's arrest, and will be pleased to hear that we now have evidence that our friend, Denny, who is with us tonight, was abducted and held prisoner by him."

The clapping and cheering died down when Terry raised a hand and continued. "You may remember, or have read, of several murders and the disappearance of three small children more than twenty years ago...

Perry's first wife was their mother, previously Mary Bryce, who lost her first husband in a tragic accident. He was known to Perry who, within six months, married the widow and moved into her home, becoming stepfather to her children."

Skipping through what was accepted to be the abduction of the children a year or so later, and reminding everyone that Mary, had been beaten and left for dead, Terry said she had survived for a while, but was too brain-damaged to recover. "Let us imagine that her spirit lingered in the place she had last seen her children," Terry continued... "Many years later, a house was built on the same ground that her cottage had occupied. When the Fletcher family moved in, their three children being similar in age, Mary imagined that they were hers."

The audience reaction to his words was mixed. It was clear that a ghost story was not what they expected.

Terry laughed... "Just setting the mood," he explained. "When Perry heard of the 'haunting' – and don't forget that the children apparently saw and spoke with Mary's ghost – he was naturally intrigued. They were talking about his dead wife. The fact that a growling dog also featured in the haunting must have perturbed him, as we have reason to believe that he beat the dog to death."

There was much nodding and whispering at the mention of the dog. Nobody other than the children had ever seen Mary, but there were too many accounts of the growling hound to ignore. Terry said he could only guess what had made Perry volunteer to accompany the woman who was nervous about sitting. Curiosity was clearly a factor, but perhaps he felt threatened by what might be revealed.

He was clearly uneasy about his brutal treatment of the animal, but he was the type who would dismiss such things as ghosts – and how could they possibly harm him – he was no pansy to be scared of things that weren't really there!

"This is why we wanted to monitor what happened here on Saturday evening. Perry was already a person of interest to us and it was an excellent opportunity to observe his actions without any risk to the family." The air of anticipation had heightened and by this time all were eager to see the film.

They were observers from the arrival of the baby-sitters to the dramatic end of the evening and would hear every word spoken.

51. The Screening

The room was lit only by a low wattage table lamp behind Terry and all eyes were glued to the screen. The entrance hall appeared on it and the sitting room door was ajar. The camera zoomed in and out again, and then several shots in succession showed the view from the entrance hall. The kitchen door at the end of the passage was open and from the same position the whole width of the landing could be seen. The door to the children's room opened and Peggy came out. Closing it behind her she started walking downstairs.

A few minutes passed before the doorbell rang and Peggy greeted Greta. Everyone was spellbound as they witnessed next the arrival of Elvis Perry. Everything that was done or said had been recorded. Terry speeded the film through passages when nothing was happening, while Perry watched television and Greta read.

The audience could hear the football match in progress and saw Greta come out to listen for a few moments at the bottom of the stairs. They all grinned when, after she returned to the sitting room, the volume of the television was lowered.

The next hour or so showed no activity and Terry speeded things up. Perry, refreshing his drink supply, and Greta, going to fetch their supper, were witnessed by an audience with growing anticipation.

Everyone was agog when the two settled to eat and the low growls rumbled down the stairs. They grew louder, and Perry suddenly burst out into the hall. His disbelief was obvious. Eyes staring, jaw dropped, he gripped the banister and put one foot on the stairs.

The next shot was upwards from the entrance hall. They all gasped, astonished, when they saw a huge dog crouching on the landing. The snarling dog moved towards Perry and he shook, visibly. The view changed, and they saw man and dog in the same shot, from above. Perry looked wild and angry as he hissed, "*You*, Butcher... I beat you once and can do it again ...you don't scare me...!"

At that moment the view changed. Again, they were looking up, as a determined but wobbly Perry climbed the stairs. The dog snarled and crouched, about to spring, when, beyond it, a door opened. Moonlight haloed the woman in white. Her gown flowed around her as she stepped forward, her arms raised. Perry stood and gazed, horrified. "Mary? ...*Mary*..."

"*Oh Elvis... How could you...?*" She moved towards him, weeping.

Already distracted and confused, Elvis was not prepared for what happened next. He released his hold on the stair rail and screamed as the dog sprang at him. He fell backwards down the stairs. The crash of his bouncing into the hall table resounded and all who watched gasped with alarm. The next view was from above and after a few moments when they could see Elvis in a heap near the door, they saw Greta emerge from the room to find him.

Her face was not visible, but her stillness indicated shock. It was no surprise to anyone when she fainted.

For a few moments as the screen emptied and the room darkened, all who had watched sat stunned into silence. Then everyone started talking at once.

"What happened?"

"Where is the dog?"

"Have we really seen Mary's ghost?"

There were questions on all sides.

Terry said they could all make up their own minds about what they'd seen. Whether faked or not, it had the desired effect on Perry. He had drunk enough during the evening to loosen his tongue and Terry was confident that they could build up a case against him for the attack on his wife.

There was no doubt in his own mind that he could present a reasonable case for digging up the well, but this wasn't the time or place to go into that.

52. After the Show Was Over

Terry was eager to hear what Sarah thought of his presentation and it was clear that she wanted to talk to him. Naturally, the Fletcher family outstayed all the other guests. It must have seemed strange to them that they couldn't go home, it being still in police possession.

Terry assured them that he and Theo would remove all the equipment first thing in the morning. Another team would be there to clean up, so Pete and Peggy could return home in the afternoon.

Polly, ever practical, wanted to know who had edited the film and was responsible for the special effects.

There was no doubt in her mind that the ghostly woman and dog were faked but apart from laughing and saying it was a lucky thing that Perry had partaken freely of what was on offer, Terry offered no explanation, saying it was too late to go into details but he would when he came to tea tomorrow! "You will be baking again won't you?" Muttering *Cheeky young whippersnapper* under her breath, Polly couldn't help smiling.

Sarah relaxed at last and congratulated Terry on his whole performance. He said that Theo had been fantastic, not only helping him to set up the film but it was he who had advised about the choice of dog and woman they should use. He had known Mary and Butcher and there was no doubt that Perry had recognised both. Sarah gave him a strange look and shook her head. "What's wrong Sarah? Our plan worked didn't it?" Before she could answer, Theo joined them to say he had just about finished collecting their stuff together.

"I'm not sure what you want to do about the dog-handler though – he's been on the 'phone again."

"He's worried about the report I might put in. When he rings again, tell him not to worry – what happened was beyond his control." The look Terry gave Sarah told her that he was as aware as she was herself that Butcher had appeared in person!

There had been no reason for the rest of the guests to comment as they knew that Theo had known Perry's dog and chosen one that could double for it. Polly looked from one to the other as they talked and could scarcely believe that they had really filmed a ghost!

Sarah saw Polly's reaction and immediately warned her that this should never be spoken of again. The Fletchers would be horrified. They must continue to believe that the dog left with Mary. She immediately felt the presence of Mary, and Geoff, and knew that they would make sure that the animal would leave with them.

Terry, realising that the secret was out, said, "I must say that, at the time, I was furious. The film was running, Perry was at the bottom of the stairs and the handler couldn't make his dog stay in position. The dog was crawling forward one minute and the next he jumped up and ran, howling." He shook his head... "It was a bad moment, but the film was still rolling, and I saw another dog there, snarling even louder. It was amazing, and we caught it all on camera."

"What happened to the real dog?" Polly wanted to know. "I suppose you still have the footage of its reaction on the bits you spliced out..."

"I might show you one day," Terry smiled. "But the handler was as shaken as the dog. They cuddled each other in the spare bedroom and afterwards the man couldn't drag him onto the landing again – he had to carry the shivering animal out to his van!"

Theo was proud to tell them that Denny, who had also been familiar with both dogs, had been the first to congratulate them. He was astonished, particularly with the ghost of Mary. He declared that not only was she perfect in face and form but, unmistakeably her voice was Mary's. Having at last talked themselves out, Sarah decided it was time to change the subject, just a little.

"But we don't know what happened after the filming stopped." Polly protested. "Greta collapsed in a heap and presumably Elvis was taken to hospital..."

"Quite correct," Terry smiled, "but there is little else to tell. Greta was fine and still has no idea that the police were already in the house when she fainted. She just assumed that they arrived while she was unconscious and was walked back home by a policewoman, who handed her the envelope Mrs Fletcher had left with me – her sitting fee – and Perry was not badly injured, so after a bit of patching up we charged him with abducting Mr Davies and put him in a cell. We know we can make that charge stick and it will give us time to look at, and prove, all the crimes that motivated the kidnapping. Ironically, taking Denny has done more towards reopening the old unsolved cases than anything else he could have done, so now we can look at every one of his alleged victims and see what we can prove... We have quite a formidable list now."

On their way to bed, they were almost too tired to chat. It was difficult to believe that all had gone smoothly, and they need not worry about anything now... Sarah added a fervent prayer that she hoped not.

Almost immediately she had a vision of a newspaper headline...

Airplane wing falls from sky just after dawn ...
Crashes through roof in quiet Oxfordshire village.
Two dead.

Now, her prayers were for Theo and his friends, Enid and Edward Brown. She hoped that she would somehow find the right words to comfort him. Being psychic was not easy and carried the responsibility of choosing wisely what to pass on.

In this case, had the inevitable accident been attached to the house, or to Theo's unfortunate friends? Were they doomed to be killed by the falling aircraft wing wherever they slept? Or would the wing have fallen on the house while they survived on the estate, if Theo had not persuaded them to move away?

Not all warning visions could be ignored, otherwise warnings would be pointless, but who could say for certain?

Sarah didn't mention the image to Polly. There was always the possibility that neither she nor Theo would learn of the tragedy. It was a private plane from a small airfield...

Following her own advice, she put it out of her mind and hoped for the best.

53. Once Bitten

During the following week when the excitement had died down a little, Clarrie and Del with baby and Daxy, came to visit them and stayed overnight ...there was too much news to exchange over the phone.

Emma was a joy to be with. Now walking and with her small vocabulary growing, it was obvious that she was inquisitive and a fast learner. Either Sarah or Polly watched her constantly giving her parents precious time together.

When they took her out in her pushchair, with Daxy of course, it was lovely to see how the little Dachshund stayed close to her when others approached. He romped away in the open park but hurtled back to Emma whenever anyone stopped by her pushchair to chat.

When they returned home Clarrie and Del were listening to some of her old records. "I'd like to take some of these back with me, if you wouldn't mind," Clarrie asked and, of course, Sarah didn't. Their tastes in music differed!

Polly hastened to bring the tea-trolley, laden with the fruits of her early morning labour and they settled down to catch up on each other's news. When they heard about all the things that preceded the arrest of Elvis Perry, Clarrie was amazed that her mother hadn't kept her up to date with what was happening.

Sarah pointed out that until a short while ago his crimes were not proven, so it wouldn't have been wise, or fair, to blacken his name. They had so many questions to ask, especially about the film Terry had made. When they heard about the ghostly hound having to take over when the real one backed out, they couldn't help laughing.

"What about your ghost-hunting expedition," Polly asked, with an apologetic glance at Sarah, who, she knew, had enough uninvited visitors from the spirit world and didn't approve of seeking them out.

"Well," Clarrie said, "we went to a few well-known sites, like Minster Lovell and Rollright Stones, but with people wandering about it was difficult to concentrate."

She hesitated a moment and then seemed to come to a decision. "I wasn't sure whether to tell you or not – it might never happen again!"

Both Sarah and Polly looked at Clarrie, alarmed.

"Nothing bad," Clarrie hastened to say. "It might be a 'one off' but, at the Stones, I saw a woman standing alone. She turned, smiled, and spoke to me. She must have been thirty-feet away, but it was as if she had whispered in my ear." It was then that realisation dawned ...the woman was a ghostly vision.

Clarrie was obviously thrilled but didn't quite believe it. "I think at some time in the past I have seen ghosts – and certainly have seen places as they used to be – you remember, I once painted a landscape, the scene of a murder as nobody else saw it, and someone tried to kill me; I ended up in hospital."

"How could we forget?" Polly shuddered.

"Perhaps you will see Elly one day then," Sarah smiled. She had always suspected that Clarrie was as psychic as she was herself and wondered what had held her back from recognising her gift.

"It's funny," Clarrie said. "I remember describing the bearer of Rowena's message clearly enough for her to recognise him but can't remember actually seeing him."

Sarah knew that Clarrie had always assumed that she had not taken after her but was now beginning to accept that she did.

Polly sat quietly, absorbing the impact that the revelation was having on Clarrie, but happy in the knowledge that she would always use the gift as sensibly as her mother. Del was stunned and broke the sudden silence...

"Good grief! My wife is psychic! No more staying late for a drink with the crew – and I'll have to give up all my girlfriends!" He dodged the cushion that Clarrie threw at him and the tension evaporated as they all laughed.

"So, what did the woman say," Polly asked.

"She pointed out an elderly man with a young couple and said, *'Tell Bo I'm not in pain now – I love him and want him to be happy for me.'* I felt awkward and embarrassed," Clarrie admitted, "but I walked over to him and confirmed that he was Bo. He looked startled and the young woman whispered, *'mother'*. Then Bo said the only person who ever called him that was his wife... I delivered the message and left as quickly as I could."

Sarah was happy that Clarrie had done the right

thing. Risking ridicule was part of the package.

Rowena, of course was thrilled and already planning another trip, but Clarrie was not as enthusiastic as she been before and they all suspected it would never happen... Once was enough.

54. Polly Has the Last Word

On the day that the small private plane lost its wing, at dawn, their local television and national news services were far more interested in reporting the lurid discovery of the skeletons of four dead children and a dog in an old disused well.

Terry had departed – a very happy man.

Modern DNA technology made short work of identifying the bodies and found enough evidence to link the crimes to Elvis Perry. It was a relief to the older community – Mary and Geoff Bryce were remembered with affection – but it was a shock to Perry's family.

He didn't seem to have many friends, old or new. Sarah couldn't help wondering why he had married Ellen until Polly told her what she had heard in the library... The property they'd lived in was Ellen's – inherited from her parents.

It had all been too much. Sarah was tired, she and Polly needed a holiday. Before leaving, Del had reminded her that they had a standing invitation to visit his parents in Spain. They lived near Jávea, which had everything to offer, year-round: beautiful coastline and mountain scenery, and a friendly local community. Relaxing in the Mediterranean sunshine for a while would be fantastic

- Polly was sure to agree.

There was nothing to keep them here now. It had been exhausting convincing Mary and Geoff that Elvis would be punished for killing their children, but they were now all reunited and had moved on, so the Fletcher home was no longer haunted. Elly didn't need her either and visited Clarrie less often.

She wondered, idly, as she drifted off, how long it would be before she became involved with another lost soul. She wanted personal time to become more involved in the lives of the family – especially as little Emma was developing so fast.

Thinking of her beautiful Grandchild Sarah slept and dreamed. Polly found her fast asleep and crept away quietly. If anyone deserved peace and quiet it was Sarah and, with that thought in mind, she took the 'phone off the hook and smiled.

The Ghostly Echoes Series

If you enjoyed reading "Haunting Echoes" and the rest of the "Ghostly Echoes" series then please look out for the final book Restless Echoes

GHOSTLY ECHOES

Sarah sees and hears ghosts. For her it is a normal and mostly ignored part of her daily life. She doesn't like to talk about it. Only a few close friends know. Sarah hates publicity and won't hold séances. Her ability is private and personal ...but the police know and so do the spirits who seek her help (and some ghosts, especially children, are very hard to ignore). All Sarah wants to do is to live quietly with her daughter Clarrie. However, a quiet life is difficult to achieve when the recently dead keep intruding. Worse, her daughter might also be psychic and, without realising it, is walking into danger ...so a missing woman and child may soon be the least of all their worries! Originally published as Deadly Shades of Grey,

A POISONOUS ECHO

Joyce is angry that her boss won't leave his wife, so his wife will have to be removed... one way or another!
A poisoning is planned and Joyce sets out to leave a lasting impression... then Joyce goes missing... A malevolent ghost and psychic detectives form the core

of this enjoyable stand-alone sequel to Mai Griffin's *Ghostly Echoes*. Originally published as *A Poisonous Shade of Grey*,

DANGEROUS ECHOES

A young medium arrives in the village and is soon the object of much interest. So much so that she is welcomed into the household of an elderly relative of Dan's wife Elaine. Concerned, they need to enlist help to discover if the medium is as genuine as she seems and his Aunt Polly decides to investigate. Clarrie and Sarah are too involved in their own crises to realise the risks Polly is taking and Polly is so enjoying the thrill of immersing herself in old friendships and researching past romances that she is unaware of the dangerous path she may be treading...

HAUNTING ECHOES

Clarrie is on a painting break, soaking up the atmosphere of the English Countryside, with her canvas at the ready, when she is senselessly attacked by a complete stranger... Her barely started painting is stolen from its easel and Sarah is left to put the clues together while Clarrie fights for her life on a hospital bed...

The Background to 'Ghostly Echoes'

SARAH

As the wife of a successful artist, achieving normality for Sarah Grey was never going to be as simple as it is for most of us. But with the added impact of her extra sense, giving her the ability to see and hear the dead and the strongly telepathic living, 'normal' has always been a difficult concept.

After her husband died, her loneliness was almost overwhelming as she felt surrounded only by the dead, but in the background, there was always Polly, the Grey family housekeeper for many years, to keep her company.

Soldiering on alone, as so many other widows have done, eventually allows her to assume a calm façade and a gradual acceptance of death when it comes so close to home.

Selling the old house and moving to a small apartment seems a good idea until her daughter is also widowed but her instincts are to go and live with her to help out.

She has long suspected that Clarrie might have latent psychic powers and is concerned about what could happen if Clarrie tries to cope on her own. Once the grief has softened a little, she looks forward to having laughter back in the house...

CLARRIE

As an artist's daughter it is, perhaps, not surprising that Clarrie grew up with a love for paint and canvas. Encouraged by her father to accompany him on his painting trips, she learned her trade from a master painter and plies it well. Now an up and coming artist in her own right, everything seems to have come together, until Tom is tragically involved in a crippling accident and she spends the final year of her seven-year marriage nursing her paralysed and dying husband.

After his death, devastated by her traumatic loss, Clarrie is grateful for her mother's suggestion, so Sarah gives up her original plans to buy an apartment and, instead, moves into Clarrie's home.

Being able to immerse herself in her art proves therapeutic, but the immersion is so complete that Clarrie barely notices the changes in her perception of the world around her, often blurring the reality of the present with the realities of the past and that proves dangerous... Having two psychics in the house is a recipe for trouble, even if one is trying for the "quiet life" and the other is in denial...

THE GHOSTLY ECHOES SERIES BY MAI GRIFFIN

The horrific prologue to Ghostly Echoes, launches Mai Griffin's dramatic psychic mystery series. Reflecting the darkside of the mysteries that plague the day to day life of unwilling psychic Sarah Grey and her artist daughter Clarrie Hunter, the plots twist and spiral around the edge of the reader's vision. How do they face the dilemma of trying to live normally, when everything around them isn't.

Overcoming the temptation to live in denial of their unwanted psychic abilities, Clarrie and Sarah are gradually drawn in to help solve strange problems and to resolve issues surrounding unexpected deaths

No matter where she goes, danger keeps intruding into Clarrie's life and painting is not keeping it at bay...

REVIEWS FOR 'GHOSTLY ECHOES' (THEN DEADLY SHADES OF GREY)

Publisher's Note: We sent out several review copies prior to publication. These are a few of the comments on 'Deadly Shades of Grey' that we received from our first three reviewers:-

1 - I received the book at 5pm and started reading it that evening, I couldn't put it down and I certainly couldn't sleep, until I finished it at three in the morning!

2 - I usually read a book for five or ten minutes, last thing at night, before I go to sleep - I never have time to read in the day, but night after night, until I finished it, I found an hour had gone by, I was so absorbed.

3 - I thoroughly enjoyed this book, it kept me gripped til the end. I cannot wait until Book Two.

As publishers, we feel that this book never loses momentum, every page is a cliff-hanger and everyone who has read it has thoroughly enjoyed it. Available by order from all mainstream UK Book retailers.

"Deadly Shades of Grey" A gripping page-turner writes Barbara Power, (Spain). The creativity of some artists, it seems, just cannot be contained or constrained within the limits of one particular medium, and so it is with the internationally-acclaimed painter, Mai Griffin. In the first of her series which introduces the Grey family, she has turned her artistic talent to the written word and proves as adept with her pen as she is with a paint brush.

For widow Sarah Grey, who only wants to live a quiet life, being psychic is a cause of much anxiety and discomfort. However, she knows that to maintain her peace of mind and sanity she must force herself to respond to the messages that haunt her. Adding to Sarah's anxiety is the fact that her daughter, Clarrie, seems to have inherited the same psychic ability, a situation which could lead her into terrible danger

Deadly Shades of Grey is a well-crafted mystery/murder novel with a gripping and taut plot that has intriguing twists and turns. It is a good and thoroughly satisfying read. Although Book 1 is a stand-alone novel, I cannot wait to get hold of Book 2 to learn more about this interesting family and what happens to them.

About Mai Griffin

During her successful career as an artist (www.maigriffin.com), travelling the world and painting portraits of Royalty and other prominent figures, Mai has never stopped writing. The Echoes series may be built around purely fictional characters, but Sarah Grey and her late husband Stephen were inspired by Mai's parents. Mai now lives in Spain. Dividing her time between painting and writing is a challenge, but helps to still her own ghosts...

by Mai Griffin

Renaming an already published book series was a heart-wrenching decision – the contents of the books and the stories have not changed, however, so for your convenience and that of booksellers the new and the old titles are below

Deadly Shades of Grey is now 'Ghostly Echoes'
A Poisonous Shade of Grey is now 'A Poisonous Echo'
Grey Masque of Death is now 'Dangerous Echoes'
Haunting Shades of Grey is now 'Haunting Echoes'
'Restless Echoes' is the last in the series

Somebody Came (Stand-alone)

Follow Mai on **www.maiwriting.com**